'Look after me for a couple of weeks and I'll set you free.'

'What do you mean, set me free?' Poppy asked.

Orsino's mouth curled up at one side. 'That should be obvious. I'll give you a divorce.'

Poppy stared. Was he offering an easy divorce because that was what he wanted or because he thought she did?

'Why should I go to such bother when I could just visit a lawyer and file for divorce?'

He didn't like that. She saw his mouth tighten.

'Because I have it in my power to make divorce easy…' He paused. 'Or hard. You get to choose whether it's smooth and painless or drawn out and very, very public.'

No mistaking the threat in the rough velvet timbre of his voice. Silence throbbed between them, fraught with vulnerabilities she'd thought she'd conquered years ago and a challenge she didn't dare refuse.

A divorce would free her, make her whole. She'd thought herself free of Orsino, but her reaction today had taught her otherwise. Despite the way he'd shattered her dreams, some remnant of emotion remained.

It was a remnant she was determined to obliterate.

'You've got yourself a deal, Orsino. I'll give you a couple of weeks for old times' sake and then I never want to see you again.'

*Step into the opulent glory of the world's most elite hotel,
where clients are the impossibly rich
and exceptionally famous.*

*Whether you're in America, Australia, Europe or Dubai,
our doors will always be open...*

Welcome to

The Chatsfield

Synonymous with style, sensation... and scandal!

For years, the children of Gene Chatsfield—
global hotel entrepreneur—have shocked the world's media
with their exploits. But no longer! When Gene appoints a
new CEO, Christos Giatrakos, to bring his children into
line, little does he know what he's starting.

Christos's first command scatters the Chatsfields
to the furthest reaches of their international holdings—
from Las Vegas to Monte Carlo, Sydney to San Francisco...
But will they rise to the challenge set by a man
who hides dark secrets in his past?

Let the games begin!

Your room has been reserved, so check in to enjoy
all the passion and scandal we have to offer.

Ref: 00106875

www.thechatsfield.com

The Chatsfield

SHEIKH'S SCANDAL, Lucy Monroe
PLAYBOY'S LESSON, Melanie Milburne
SOCIALITE'S GAMBLE, Michelle Conder
BILLIONAIRE'S SECRET, Chantelle Shaw
TYCOON'S TEMPTATION, Trish Morey
RIVAL'S CHALLENGE, Abby Green
REBEL'S BARGAIN, Annie West
HEIRESS'S DEFENCE, Lynn Raye Harris

8 volumes to collect—you won't want to miss out!

REBEL'S BARGAIN

BY
ANNIE WEST

Published in Great Britain 2014
by Mills & Boon, an imprint of Harlequin (UK) Limited,
Eton House, 18-24 Paradise Road, Richmond, Surrey, TW9 1SR

© 2014 Harlequin Books S.A.

Special thanks and acknowledgement are given to Annie West
for her contribution to *The Chatsfield* series

ISBN: 978-0-263-24329-1

Annie West has devoted her life to an intensive study of tall, dark, charismatic heroes who cause the best kind of trouble in the lives of their heroines. As a sideline she's also researched dream-worthy locations for romance, from bustling, vibrant cities to desert encampments and fairytale castles. It's hard work but she loves a challenge.

Annie lives with her family at beautiful Lake Macquarie, on Australia's east coast. She loves to hear from readers and you can contact her at www.annie-west.com or at PO Box 1041, Warners Bay, NSW 2282, Australia.

Recent titles by the same author:

DAMASO CLAIMS HIS HEIR
  (One Night with Consequences)
AN ENTICING DEBT TO PAY
  (At His Service)
IMPRISONED BY A VOW
CAPTIVE IN THE SPOTLIGHT

Did you know these are also available as eBooks?
Visit www.millsandboon.co.uk

DEDICATION/ACKNOWLEDGEMENT

To all the other 'Chatsfield Girls'
with thanks for the laughter and support.
It's been fantastic working with you all.

CHAPTER ONE

'I'LL BE THERE as soon as I can organise flights.'

Orsino heard an unfamiliar grim note in his brother's voice. News your twin had almost died would sober anyone. He grimaced.

After years of risk-taking his luck had run out. Being faced with his own mortality and possible permanent incapacity was forcing him to reassess his life.

'There's no need to race here, Lucca.' He shifted the phone and winced as he knocked the bandages on his head. 'There's nothing you can do. Besides—' he forced a smile into his voice '—you'd spend your time flirting with the nurses and ignoring me.'

'How can you say that?' No mistaking Lucca's relief at Orsino's joke. 'I'm a changed man. There's only one woman for me and she's a real princess.'

Orsino groaned at his brother's awful pun. Lucca's romance with a royal hadn't improved his sense of humour.

'Besides, the nurses probably have their hands full with you,' Lucca continued. 'Have you got a date with the prettiest one yet?'

Orsino swallowed the retort that he had no idea what the staff looked like. That was a detail not even Lucca needed to know. Unless it became absolutely necessary.

'You're the lady-killer, Lucca, remember?'

'This is me you're talking to, Orsino. I've seen how women react to you. Not that I could work out why, when

I'm the handsome twin. You're seriously saying you're not fending women off?'

'Not right at the moment.'

Orsino gritted his teeth against swamping self-pity and anger. Not anger at Lucca, but at the disaster his world had become. The staff fussed over him only because it had been touch and go at first whether he'd survive.

'Of course.' Lucca sounded serious again. 'That's why one of us should be there. You need family.'

'Family!' Orsino didn't hide his bitterness.

The closest family had come recently was when his father's CEO, Christos Giatrakos, had made contact, wanting to cash in on Orsino's reputation, requesting—no, demanding—that he be the 'face' of the company. Orsino and his father had never been close but at least the old man could have rung himself.

'Yeah, well, I know I've been busy but—'

'I didn't mean you, Lucca.' Orsino palmed his bristled jaw with his unbandaged hand, feeling like an ungrateful heel. 'Sorry. I'm in a foul mood, not used to being stuck in a hospital bed. I shouldn't take it out on you.' He drew a slow breath, knowing his injuries were only part of the problem. 'I appreciate the offer but there's nothing you can do here.'

'Maybe not now, but when you're released from hospital you'll need someone.'

'You're offering to play nurse?' Orsino smiled. 'It might be worth agreeing just to see it.'

His twin's chuckle was the best thing he'd heard in days, warming him in ways thermal blankets hadn't. Orsino hadn't realised till this week what was important in his life. Now he knew, and he'd make it his business to catch up with his twin more regularly. But only after he'd recovered enough not to be a figure of sympathy.

'Why do you always underestimate me, Orsino? Just because you're a couple of minutes older?'

'I'm picturing you in a starched cap and apron, Lucca.

The idea has a certain appalling fascination.' Orsino spoke again over his brother's laugh. 'Don't worry about the nurse-maid gig. I've lined up someone.'

'Lucilla?'

'No, though she called. Our big sister still worries about us after all these years, and despite the fact Giatrakos clearly runs her ragged.'

'You need someone experienced, someone you can trust.'

Orsino bit back a bark of laughter. *Trust?*

No, trust didn't describe his feelings for Poppy. Once he'd vowed never to see her again. But days stuck on a mountain expecting to die gave him a new perspective.

He'd never trust her again. But there was a freedom, and power, in knowing that.

Poppy and he had unfinished business. That's why she still haunted his thoughts. For five years he'd told himself he was done with the past, but in the burst of clarity that had come to him on the mountainside, he knew it would never be over till he'd faced her one more time.

Something lingered there. Something he had to face before he walked away for ever.

She'd hate being with him again. After what she'd done that would be tough, even for a woman so brazen. As for being at his beck and call while he recovered...

Orsino's lips curved in a tight smile. He looked forward to making her squirm. It was small enough revenge for what she'd done.

'Don't fret, Lucca. The woman I have in mind is just what the doctor ordered.'

Poppy drew a jagged breath as the taxi wove through traffic.

Fear had crowded close from the moment news broke of the avalanche and the two injured climbers. Even strangers felt fear for Orsino and awe for what he'd done. She'd over-heard them discussing it at the airport: Orsino Chatsfield's heroism, or his foolhardiness, depending on your view.

She looked at her ringless hands twisting in her lap. It wasn't fear she felt but terror. It grated through her empty stomach.

She hadn't seen Orsino in five years but she couldn't imagine a world without him in it. His vitality, his passion, oh, Lord, his passion!

Her hands clenched as memories rushed to the surface, heating her skin.

His arrogance. His demands. The way he was so ready to judge but so unready to face his own faults.

Despite all the negatives, a hard, heavy lump pressed down on her chest as if she'd swallowed an anvil.

The message from the hospital—so uninformative, yet so peremptory—had congealed the dread in her veins. It had sent her racing from France to the base of the Himalayas. She hadn't caught her breath the whole way. Even now her heart pumped too fast.

The taxi stopped and Poppy looked out at the ugly hospital, her heart in her mouth.

She didn't even blink when a cluster of press surged, bombarding her with questions. She barely heard them. All she could think of was what awaited her inside.

Poppy's footsteps echoed in the silent corridor. With each step her nerves screwed tighter.

Please, please. Let him survive. Let him live.

She'd told herself she felt nothing for Orsino Chatsfield. The burn of negative feelings had died long ago, buried under the overload of sheer hard work that had taken her to the top of her profession. No time to feel hurt, regret or guilt when every waking hour was occupied. That's what she'd told herself for five years. What she'd believed. Till yesterday.

The fact he'd almost died on one of the world's inhospitable mountains, might even now be dying, made her swallow convulsively, her throat clogging.

He couldn't die.

Poppy stumbled. She who never faltered, not even in six-inch stilettos, navigating a catwalk artistically obscured by dry-ice vapour.

Finally she reached the last room. Taking a shaky breath she stepped in, only to halt as she spied the figure unmoving in the hospital bed.

He was so still that for a horrible few seconds she wondered if he breathed.

Poppy pressed her hand to her chest. Her heart battered her ribs so hard it felt like it might jump free.

Her gaze riveted on the bed. She couldn't remember Orsino being still. He was always on the move, as if his life force was greater than everyone else's. The only time she'd seen him unmoving was when she'd woken before him. She remembered drinking in the sight of him, heart-stoppingly gorgeous, so precious as he sprawled beside her. The desperate intensity of her feelings had terrified her.

With good reason.

She should have trusted her instincts and run for her life. Except she'd been hooked from the first look.

Orsino lay swathed in bandages—glaring white against his tan. One arm was in a sling, covered from fingers to elbow. The other, bare on the cotton blanket, bore livid bruises. His head was bandaged, as well. Not just his scalp but his eyes, too.

Poppy's heart plunged to the toes of her soft kid boots.

Only the darkened jawline and column of bronzed throat were familiar. They were strong, beautifully formed and powerful. And his mouth—she surveyed those thin lips that could quirk in a smile guaranteed to make a woman's heart soar.

She blinked, trying not to remember the words that had shot from those sculpted lips five years ago. But time hadn't diminished her memory. They slashed her anew, reviving guilt, indignation and tearing pain.

Poppy swallowed convulsively. How bad *was* he? The news reports had been sensational but unreliable. Those head wounds—

'Amindra? Is that you?'

Everything in her froze at the low words, gravelly as if he wasn't used to speaking. She remembered that early-morning voice, how it had woken her so often, murmuring outrageous suggestions as his marauding hands played her body like a maestro tuning an instrument.

Relief flooded her that he was well enough to speak, and horror, too, at her tumbling rush of emotions.

Poppy bit her cheek, summoning strength. She felt wobbly but after more than a decade modelling she was an expert at hiding behind an impassive mask.

Her gaze went to his bandaged eyes and she shivered. Fear iced her spine.

'Nurse?' His voice was sharper. 'Is that you?'

'Hello, Orsino.' Her voice was like smooth, golden honey, as rich and seductive as in his dreams.

He stiffened, fingers stilling as they groped for the call button. He registered the familiar disinfectant hospital scent and realised this was no dream.

Something whacked him hard in the chest, a jolt of pain as his bruised ribs expanded then eased when he remembered to breathe again.

She'd come.

Even trussed up like a turkey dinner and blind to boot, he knew her voice. He'd know it anywhere. He'd even thought he'd heard it beneath half a tonne of snow. It had bullied and cajoled him into not giving up. How was that for ironic? He must have been out of his mind.

'Who is it?'

Orsino heard her soft gasp. Obviously she expected him to recognise her voice but he'd be damned if he'd give her that satisfaction.

She'd come too soon! They'd promised to take the bandages off his eyes today. He hadn't wanted her seeing him like this—helpless and light-headed from medication that kept pain to a dull throb.

How had she got here so fast when he wasn't expecting her for another couple of days?

'It's Poppy.' She was at the end of the bed.

'Poppy?' His voice thickened unexpectedly on the second syllable, turning it into a question. Orsino flinched, detesting the emotion he heard in that single word. Where had that come from?

Heat flared under his skin and he knew in his gut it wasn't just hurt pride because she saw him like this—*so much less than the man he'd been*. It was something blood-deep and disturbing. Something he no longer wanted to feel.

He'd finally acknowledged they had loose ends to tie up but nothing had prepared him for the explosion of unwanted emotion her presence ignited.

Had he made a mistake, getting her here?

It wouldn't be his first where she was concerned.

'Yes, it's me.' Her voice came from right beside him. 'How are you?'

Orsino groped for the bed controls. He hated being flat on his back while she hovered over him. Bad enough with the nurses…

'Let me. What did you want?' Soft fingers brushed his and he jerked away. He told himself it was because he didn't like the pity in her voice. The tingling in his fingers was a legacy of frostbite, no more.

'Orsino?'

His lips compressed as his body responded to her husky whisper. It reminded him of the last time they'd been together. The memory caught him up short, smashing his composure.

Damn! This wasn't supposed to happen.

'I can do it myself.' This time when he reached for the

controls her hand was gone. Seconds later he was sitting up, the bed supporting him.

He shifted his weight, trying to get comfortable.

'Here, I can help.' No huskiness this time. Just cool efficiency. Orsino told himself he welcomed it.

Then the scent of raspberries reached him—tangy and sweet—and she tugged the pillows behind him so he sat more comfortably. Something soft brushed his jaw and he reached up, catching it.

It was a lock of hair. Soft and springy, tickling his palm, twisting around his finger. He tugged lightly and felt warmth surround him, as if she'd leaned close. The light raspberry-and-woman scent deepened in his nostrils and he swallowed hard as the past rose in a consuming wave.

He told himself to release his grip but his hold tightened on the silk skein of her hair. He tried to imagine it cascading in dark red waves around her pale shoulders and was disturbed to find he pictured it too clearly.

'You've grown your hair.' The whole time he'd known her it had been gamine short. Poppy's air of youthful fragility, reinforced by her stunning eyes in that sculpted face, had caught the public's imagination. She'd been the fresh, innocently sexy face of fashion.

Innocent!

His mouth twisted as tension knotted his chest and belly.

'I wanted a new look.' Her words sounded offhand.

Orsino released her. He refused to ask if her *new look* dated from their separation. For five years he'd avoided society pages and magazines that might feature her. Now wasn't the time for curiosity to reawaken.

Nor his libido.

But it had. Even battered and bruised, his body responded to her feminine scent and the sound of her voice. Too eagerly. Sex hadn't been part of his plan. It infuriated him that she could still do this to him.

He leaned back against the pillows, increasing the distance between them. Yet the perfume of her skin lingered.

When he'd imagined them meeting he'd envisaged himself almost healed, enough to see at least.

His jaw tightened. It had been a mistake mentioning her name so soon to the officious hospital staff. He should have waited. He hated not being in control.

'How do you feel, Orsino?'

A laugh grated in his throat. 'What? You were worried about me?'

She didn't answer but he felt new tension in the air. Something that made him sit straighter. He sensed her turmoil and his predatory senses twitched. How he wished he could see her!

'The whole world is wondering how you are. You're an international hero for saving your climbing partner and yourself.'

'Ah, that's why you came running so quickly. To bask in the reflected media glow.' Everywhere they'd gone, whenever he'd wanted privacy, there'd been someone with a camera wanting pictures of them, dubbed by some trashy magazine the year's hottest couple. He'd been slow to realise it was attention Poppy, with her need for constant media coverage, wanted.

'I see you haven't changed, Orsino.' Her voice came from farther away and held a razor-sharp edge. 'Still the charmer. And still so quick to judge us lesser mortals.'

He ignored that. What was there to say? He'd been in the right. She'd been in the wrong, so far in the wrong he'd known a moment of red-hot fury when violence would have been a welcome outlet. Lucky for Poppy Graham he was a civilised man. Some men wouldn't have walked away as he had. Some would have taken revenge for what she'd done.

Having her at his beck and call for a couple of weeks while he recuperated hardly counted.

'Have *you* changed, Poppy?' This time when he spoke

her name the word emerged crisp and clear, yet he tasted the echo of it on his tongue, sweet as wild raspberries but with a tang of disappointment.

How was it that after all this time she had the power to make him *feel*?

It must be some residual weakness after his ordeal in the wilderness.

'Of course I've changed.' He heard her long stride across the floor as she paced. 'I'm not twenty-three any more. I'm my own woman, self-reliant, secure and capable.'

'You were always self-reliant,' he murmured. 'You never needed anyone, did you, Poppy? Except on your own terms.' He heard her hiss of breath. 'You used people for what you could get. Is that still your style?'

'You're a fine one to talk! When did you ever *give* or share?' Orsino heard her jagged breath and knew intense satisfaction that he wasn't the only one *feeling*.

'I remember giving all the time.' He breathed deep. 'Money, the prestige and connections you were so hungry for...'

Silence met his accusation. He waited, but she didn't break it.

So, in one thing at least she'd changed. Once she'd been ruled by passion, as impetuous in her defence as in everything else. Now she knew when to give up. What was the point arguing the unwinnable?

Orsino frowned, fighting a disappointment he couldn't explain.

'Obviously you don't want me here.' Her voice sounded guarded and, if he hadn't known it impossible, defeated. 'The hospital made a mistake contacting me.'

He shook his head, wishing yet again that he could see her face. The strength of his need to see her stunned him.

'No mistake. But they were a little too prompt. You're not needed quite yet.'

'Needed? You don't need me.'

Orsino heard the shock in her voice and didn't bother hiding his smile. Maybe it was shallow of him but after all this time, after what she'd done, it felt good to have her exactly where he wanted her.

'But when I leave hospital I will. Who else should look after me as I recuperate but my wife?'

CHAPTER TWO

'WIFE?' POPPY'S VOICE ROSE. 'You're kidding!'

But looking at his satisfied smile she had a dreadful feeling Orsino wasn't joking. There were new lines around his mouth, grim lines that hadn't been there when she'd known him. They spoke of rock-hard determination. And pain.

She blinked as her heart squeezed. How bad *were* his injuries? He still hadn't told her. Those bandaged eyes...

Poppy pulled herself up. Did she seriously think she could read Orsino when so much of his face was swathed in bandages?

He was a stranger now. He'd severed any connection.

'Why should I kid?'

It was there in his voice now, that smugness. As if he enjoyed her reaction, knowing her discomfort. The realisation made her shiver.

Orsino had been hard, unreasonable and unforgiving. But spinning out a painful situation hadn't been his style. He'd preferred to walk away, leaving her bereft.

Had he changed?

'Because I'm not your wife. You can't want me nursing you.'

'It won't be full-time nursing. I expect to manage once the bandages come off.' Was that a hint of doubt in his voice? But he was talking again, distracting her from the fleeting impression. 'I'll only need someone on hand to be sure. That's where you come in.'

'As I said, Orsino, I'm not your wife. It won't be me caring for you. Ask someone else.'

Then a horrible thought struck. Had his head injury affected his memory? Didn't he recall what had happened between them? Poppy swayed. The possibility of brain damage was too much on top of exhaustion.

'Of course you're my wife. You never filed for divorce.' He paused. 'Why is that, Poppy? Because there was still publicity to be milked from my name?'

His icy tone grazed her skin, making her shudder.

Relief battered her, and anger. No memory loss after all. Orsino recalled everything. And still blamed her.

Poppy stiffened her backbone, setting her jaw and telling herself she'd been a fool to think he'd ever be glad to see her.

She didn't want this man in her life. She was *glad* to be rid of him.

Yet his question rang in her ears. Why hadn't she divorced him?

'You didn't file for divorce, either.' Poppy stopped, hating how scratchy and thin her voice sounded, revealing her turmoil. She breathed deep, clasping her hands before her. They trembled.

Orsino had always made her feel too deeply.

Time hadn't cauterised the wounds at all. She'd just pretended it had. That knowledge scared her as nothing had in years.

'Our marriage ended when you walked out.' Though it had taken her far longer to realise it. The memory of her desperate hopes and frantic phone calls, all unanswered, made her itch with embarrassment.

'When I walked out? Talk about selective memory!' Orsino shook his head. 'There's no mistake. I gave the hospital your name.'

Poppy blinked owlishly at the man before her. He'd orchestrated this?

She darted a glance towards the door. Why stay and let him manipulate her?

Yet something welded her to the spot. Pity for his injuries? Better that than the alternative, that somewhere, deep down, she still cared. That she didn't want to leave till she found out how badly he was hurt and whether he'd see again.

'You had no business giving them my name.'

He shrugged and Poppy hated herself for noticing the way his broad shoulders moved against the white bed linen, as if she were some love-struck teenager, transfixed by his athletic physique.

Been there, got the T-shirt, over it now.

If only she believed it. The thread of unexpected heat twisting deep inside belied her certainty.

'The hospital needed my next of kin. That's you, Poppy. It has been ever since we left that registry office together.'

She shook her head. 'What about Lucca? What about Lucilla? You've got all those brothers and sisters. Plus your father. Any one of them—'

'They're all tied up at the moment. Besides, by law you're my next of kin.'

'And you thought *I* wouldn't be busy?' Her hands slipped to her hips as anger hiked. 'Unlike you, I have to work for my living. I'm in the middle of a photo shoot. I can't simply drop everything to nurse you.'

'But you just did, didn't you?' His words punctured her fury, pulling her up short. Poppy bit her lip, the salt tang of blood filling her mouth.

He was right. She'd thrown over everything in the rush to get to him.

Would she have a job to return to? There'd been talk of working around her absence, shooting without her for a few days, but she'd barely taken it in.

Poppy chewed her lip. Of course she'd have a job. Hers was the new face of Baudin.

But she'd left them in the lurch. Never had she behaved

so. Poppy Graham was always a consummate professional, punctual and reliable. Until now. She spun on her heel and marched to the window, pushing her hair back over a shoulder that slumped with weariness.

Looking up she saw the dark bulk of the Himalayas, enormous as a crouching giant. Her heart plunged at the thought of what might have happened.

'What were you doing up there?' She shivered and wrapped her arms around her middle, wishing she could warm the part of her that was still frozen from lingering fear. 'You must have known it was ridiculously dangerous, especially at this time of year!'

'Why, Poppy, if I didn't know better I'd almost believe you were worried about me.'

She swung around, fingers biting into her arms through her cashmere sweater. 'Spare me the act, Orsino. I'm not in the mood.' She breathed deep. 'Much as I…dislike you, I never wished you dead.'

His tight smile disappeared. The lines bracketing his mouth scored deeper than she remembered. What was the rest of his face like beneath those bandages? Grim like his mouth?

'Really? But you'd look superb in widow's weeds.' His voice grated on stretched nerves. 'You'd do stoic vulnerability with such panache. Think of all the lovely media sympathy to boost your profile.'

She strode to his bed, slamming to a stop beside him. 'That's a vile thing to say! I never…' She swallowed hard, choking on a fiery ball of tangled emotion. 'You can be an absolute bastard, did you know that?'

His mouth thinned. 'So I've been told.'

No doubt by some woman. Poppy swung away but stopped as long fingers closed unerringly around her wrist.

How had he known so precisely where she was when he couldn't see her?

The warm abrasiveness of his callused fingers held her

in a familiar grasp. She told herself she felt only fury at his accusations.

Yet it wasn't true. She repressed a shudder as her nerve cells leapt in recognition of his touch. Memory bombarded her. Orsino's hand linking with hers as the marriage celebrant pronounced them husband and wife. His hand splayed at the back of her head as he tilted his face to hers the first time they kissed. His hand trawling in slow seduction over her naked body.

Even through the pervasive smell of hospital cleansers she caught the scent of his skin. She drew it in hungrily. She'd missed it, she realised, that subtle tang of cedar wood spiced with something that was wholly, uniquely Orsino.

His thumb swiped the inside of her wrist, over the spot where her pulse raced. It felt like a caress.

She tugged her hand but his fingers closed tight. Despite his injuries he was physically stronger.

Once, she'd revelled in his strength that made her feel fragile and feminine despite her almost six feet in height. Orsino had made her feel delicate instead of gangly. His embrace had awakened Cinderella fantasies she'd harboured as a child, before the harsh realities of life cured her of believing in happy-ever-afters. In his arms she'd actually believed that they might come true after all.

'Let me go, Orsino.' Miraculously her voice was composed.

For a second longer he held her, almost as if he didn't want to release her.

Then she was free. She took a step back, her other hand circling her wrist, covering the place where his heat lingered.

'What were you doing up on the mountain, Orsino? Everyone said it was a dangerous climb.'

'Danger is part of the appeal.'

'That's no answer.' She'd never understood his need to

fling himself into one perilous venture after another. 'Even by your standards this was foolhardy.'

'Not foolhardy. A calculated risk. Ice climbing always is.'

'Then you didn't calculate very well, did you?' Why she harped on like this Poppy didn't know. But she couldn't leave it alone.

Even after all that had passed between them, she hated him risking his neck.

'No one could have predicted that avalanche. I'm not omniscient, you know, Poppy.'

She watched his mouth form her name and a deep tingling throb began inside. Maybe it was the way he said it, in that dark-as-night voice, but something long forgotten stirred.

Poppy took another step back from the bed.

'No one has ever done that climb, because it's so dangerous. The experts say it's impossible.'

'Only until someone does it. Besides, if we'd succeeded the money we raised would have funded a new eye clinic and helped scores of local families.'

'You risked your life for an eye clinic?' Poppy knew he raised money for charity with his more daring adventures, but this—

'Why not? Better this than as some commercial stunt for a luxury company.' His voice held an unfamiliar note and Poppy watched his hand clench on the coverlet.

'Orsino? What do you mean?'

He waved his hand dismissively. 'Nothing. What I do with my time is my business. Mine alone.'

Wasn't that the truth?

When she'd needed him, when she'd been desperate for his strong arms holding her, he'd headed off on one of his adventures. He hadn't cared enough to support her, too busy taking on the next challenge.

'It's not just your business when it endangers others.

What about your climbing partner and the men who rescued you? You were selfish to put them in danger.'

'Michael is recovering nicely down the hall. He knew the risks.' But the rough edge to Orsino's tone made her wonder if, after all, he felt guilty.

Orsino raised his hand as if to rake his fingers through his hair in a gesture of frustration she recalled too clearly. When his hand touched bandage it dropped to the bed.

'As for the rescue party—' His mouth pursed. 'We'd left instructions that no rescue was to be attempted if anything went wrong. We know how many local guides are killed and injured supporting foreign climbers.'

'It's a good thing for you they ignored your wishes.' Poppy wrapped her arms across her chest, chilled anew at the thought of Orsino on the unforgiving mountain, buried in snow. How long did it take to die from exposure?

Suddenly he grinned. With his dark stubble surrounding that slash of white teeth he looked like a pirate.

Poppy stared, telling herself it was *not* a zing of attraction she felt. That was no longer possible.

'I'm not complaining.' His smile faded. 'We knew them all from previous years here, that's why they ignored our wishes. Bloody fools. If something had happened to one of them...'

He really was the most complex, unreasonable, infuriating man.

She wanted to despise him for his life of idle luxury but he risked his life raising money for others. She wanted to berate him for taking stupid risks but he'd cold-bloodedly taken on this challenge knowing he could die and demanding no one risk their life to save him.

Poppy sank into a visitor's chair. No wonder she felt confused. Orsino Chatsfield was the sort of man to tie anyone in knots. But just because he had a social conscience didn't mean he was good husband material.

Good husband! If the idea didn't hurt so much it might have been funny.

She hadn't thought of him as her husband in ages.

Yet there was still *something* about this man that burrowed deep beneath logic and reason. Something that had squeezed her heart till she couldn't breathe when she thought he was going to die. Something that hurt like the devil when he accused her of wanting him dead.

He had the power to anger her and hurt her as no one else could.

Why hadn't that died when he killed her love?

Poppy watched her hands twist in her lap and knew real fear. Fear that, despite everything, it wasn't over between them. At least not for her.

She shook her head. It couldn't be. She was stronger than that. Five years ago she'd grovelled, leaving pleading messages for Orsino to contact her. None had been answered.

That was how little she'd meant to him.

Since then she'd dragged herself back from the brink, facing the glare of the press, the curiosity of millions, slavering for details on their breakup, probing her feelings and watching her every move.

Unlike Orsino, Poppy didn't have the buffer of extreme wealth to protect her. She'd had to get back to work, acting as if her heart hadn't been ripped into bleeding shreds.

It had taken everything she had to rebuild herself, to be more resilient and focused than before.

She lifted her head and scrutinised Orsino. He pretended he still had some say in her life, but he'd forfeited that right long ago.

He had no hold over her.

All she had to do was remember that and ignore her body's traitorous awareness of him. That must be some legacy of the past, a sense memory that would soon fade.

'Are you still there?' His deep voice broke her reverie. Was that a hint of vulnerability she heard? It would be natural given those injuries. But the set of Orsino's firm jaw spoke of strength, not fear. Why would he be concerned if she'd left? He who'd deliberately faced death on that treacherous climb?

'Why did you tell the hospital to contact me? And don't give me that line about being your next of kin.'

'I told you. I need someone to be with while I recuperate.'

Need not *want*.

Was that why his jaw set so tight? Because he didn't want her but needed her help? Yet this was Orsino Chatsfield. He didn't do anything unless it suited him.

'Why, Orsino?'

'Why not?' he shot back at her. 'Surely you owe me?'

'Owe you?' Indignation warred with guilt, just as it had all those years ago.

Her cheeks flamed at the memory of what she'd done to deserve his disgust. But at the same time anger surged. He'd never admitted his role in what had happened, never once tried to understand. If it hadn't been for his arrogance and selfish pride—

'I don't owe you a thing, Orsino.'

'So you say, but would those millions of fans agree if they knew the details of why we split?'

Poppy felt her eyes bulge.

'You're trying to *blackmail* me?' She groped for words, her brain spinning. 'Why now? Why after all this time?' It didn't make sense.

'Blackmail? To expect a wife to take care of her husband when he needs her?'

His arch tone set her teeth on edge.

'I haven't the time or inclination to continue this discussion.' She rose and picked up her bag. 'Spread what stories you like, Orsino. It makes no difference to me.'

It was a lie. Damaging rumours would make her life hell again. With photos of Orsino as a wounded hero she'd be cast as a villainess, her reputation in tatters as well as her peace. It was bound to impact on her career.

But she couldn't let it matter. Losing her self-respect was too high a price.

'Wait!'

His peremptory tone stopped her as she turned away.

'I have a proposition.'

Reluctantly she turned. What she could see of his face looked paler than before. His mouth was set in a thin line of pain. She eyed his tense jaw and wondered if she could call the nurse.

How could she feel concern for a blackmailer? It didn't make sense. But then nothing about her reactions to this man was logical.

'Poppy?'

'I'm listening.'

'I refuse to stay in a convalescent home. I want privacy while I recuperate.'

'So?' She refrained from pointing out that with his money he could buy the best medical care in his own home. 'Why not ask one of your women to look after you?'

Orsino was regularly seen with a gorgeous woman at his side, a different one every week.

'Why not this Amindra you were expecting? I'm sure she'd jump at the chance to be alone with you.'

His chuckle rippled, warm and rich, across her skin and Poppy was appalled to feel herself melt a little at the knees. Till he spoke again and her hackles rose. 'Ah, that explains your bad mood. Are you jealous?'

She stood straighter, a shaft of fury stiffening her backbone. 'Absolutely not. Now, I have a return flight to organise.'

She'd taken just one step when he spoke again. 'Amindra is a nurse. I'm sure she'd jump at the chance for extra money but not if it means leaving her children and grandchildren behind for several weeks.'

'She's a nurse?'

'Who else would I meet in this condition?' For the first time Orsino's voice betrayed bitterness as he waved his hand in a slashing gesture across his bandaged torso. It spoke of barely leashed frustration and all at once it hit her how difficult an active man like Orsino must find his forced confinement. She'd been so caught up in relief at seeing him alive, then irritation at his high-handed attitude, that hadn't sunk in.

Even badly wounded Orsino had more presence than most men she knew. If only he didn't get under her skin so!

'Look after me for a couple of weeks and I'll set you free.'

Poppy stared intently but couldn't make out his expression. Those bandages hid so much. Was he blind behind them? She wanted to ask but knew he wouldn't answer.

'What do you mean, set me free?'

His mouth curled up at one side. 'That should be obvious. I'll give you a divorce.'

Poppy's fingers tightened on the strap of her bag.

'Why now? After all this time?'

He shrugged again and fleetingly she thought of how his occasional Mediterranean gestures, the use of his hands as he spoke, the lifting of those broad shoulders, used to fascinate her. As had the intriguing combination of stunning Italian good looks and English reserve, courtesy of his Italian mother and British father.

'It's what you want, isn't it?'

Poppy stared. Was he offering an easy divorce because that's what he wanted or because he thought she did? Had he found someone else to fill the rarefied position of his wife?

For years she'd resolutely turned her thoughts away from Orsino with anyone else. Even though he wore gorgeous women like fashion accessories every time he appeared in public.

A hollow ache started up beneath her ribs. She told herself it was stress from the long journey and from facing Orsino again.

'Why should I go to such bother, when I could just visit a lawyer and file for divorce?'

He didn't like that. She saw his mouth tighten.

'Because I have it in my power to make divorce easy.' He paused. 'Or hard. You get to choose whether it's smooth and painless or drawn out and very, very public.'

No mistaking the threat in the rough velvet timbre of his voice. It was on the tip of Poppy's tongue to ask why he hadn't divorced her. But she wouldn't give him an excuse to pry into her own reasons for inaction. She hadn't worked that out herself. 'Unless—' his voice dropped to a speculative murmur '—you don't want a divorce after all?'

Silence throbbed between them, fraught with vulnerabilities she'd thought she'd conquered years ago, and a challenge she didn't dare refuse.

Divorce meant an end to their relationship. No more lingering dregs of regret, no 'if onlys' in the wakeful predawn hours.

A divorce would free her, make her whole. She'd thought herself free of Orsino but her reaction today taught her otherwise. Despite the way he'd shattered her dreams, some remnant of emotion remained.

It was a remnant she was determined to obliterate.

A couple of weeks with this arrogant, selfish man would cure her of those last hints of doubt. It would be hell but it would be worth it to finally be free.

Poppy stepped to the edge of the bed and watched him turn his head towards her.

'You've got yourself a deal, Orsino. I'll give you a couple of weeks for old times' sake and then I never want to see you again.'

CHAPTER THREE

ORSINO GRIMACED AS the doctor probed gently and pain throbbed through him.

'How long till I'm fit?' he demanded, his voice hoarse from fighting pain and the unexpected emotion of meeting Poppy just hours before.

He felt raw inside, as if the slip of deadly ice and rock had crashed right through his innards instead of merely cracking a few bones and tearing skin.

Despite his injuries, death from exposure had, by comparison, been a strangely peaceful prospect. Numbness would lead to loss of consciousness then nothing. No pain, no struggle. Only his brain hadn't let him give in. He'd heard a voice, Poppy's voice, whenever he'd wanted to give up. He'd known he couldn't just slip away until he'd finished what was between them.

'For the arm, a month or so, though you could have lingering symptoms in this hand especially. You were in the ice too long for my liking.'

The doctor scrawled another note in his report and Orsino reminded himself he was lucky he could see the movement, no matter how poorly. The prospect of blindness had terrified him. He repressed fear that this distorted vision was the best he'd ever get.

'I'd prefer that you stayed here longer.'

Orsino opened his mouth to protest but the doctor spoke again. 'I know, I know. That's not going to happen. Since you insist on leaving I'll forward a report so your doctor can keep an eye on you. In the meantime you need rest and plenty of it.'

The doctor's terseness was a welcome change. He'd grown sick of that unfailingly upbeat tone with which the nurses avoided answering questions about his recovery.

'You'll have to be careful of the ribs for some time. As for the lacerations and bruising, that's all healing nicely.'

Orsino let himself sag against the pillows.

'And my eyes?'

Orsino tried not to read significance into the pause before the doctor answered.

He'd come a long way from those hours half frozen as he dragged Michael from the avalanche. More than once he'd thought them both lost for ever.

Whatever the prognosis it was better than being another fatal statistic.

'Ah. Your vision. That's more difficult. As we discussed earlier, snow blindness usually doesn't last. But in some cases, such as yours, there can be longer-term damage. The injury to your head hasn't helped.'

'But I will recover?'

Again that pause. Orsino drew a deep breath as he fought panic. These days of darkness had been the most taxing of his life. How would he cope if poor vision stopped him doing the things that made life worthwhile? He'd go insane.

'I'm hopeful.'

'But?'

'But how long it takes and whether the recovery will be complete I can't say. You'll need regular monitoring. I've made a referral for you to see an excellent specialist in France.'

Orsino murmured his thanks as the doctor left.

Ironic that he'd damaged his vision while raising money for an eye clinic.

No, that wasn't true. The clinic hadn't been the real impetus for his perilous climb. It had been his father, and his own impetuous anger.

Five years ago Orsino had thrown himself into ever more reckless adventures, trying to escape the pain of loss and Poppy's betrayal.

The media had loved his dangerous stunts, providing him with an opportunity to do something he actually felt proud of—making a difference in the lives of those who needed help. His exploits lured donors to support a range of causes and for the first time he'd had real purpose, not just an easy life of privilege.

Till his father, Gene Chatsfield, took an interest.

Orsino's unbandaged hand clenched against the bed-clothes, frustration rising.

If his father had wanted to reconcile Orsino would have met him halfway.

But Gene wasn't interested in happy families. His interest was purely commercial.

Orsino gritted his teeth. Had he really hoped the old man was interested in more than making money?

To Gene Chatsfield his daredevil son was no more than a potential business asset. He wanted Orsino as the public face of his revamped luxury hotel chain, using his philanthropy as a draw card.

Heat seared Orsino's belly. His father cheapened everything Orsino had built. What had given him such purpose and satisfaction was reduced to the level of tawdry circus stunts to draw a crowd.

And when Orsino had refused he'd been threatened with loss of income from the family trust.

As if he was some callow kid, to be manipulated and brought to heel!

His father didn't know him at all. In twenty-eight years he'd learned enough about investment to build his own fortune separate from his family trust fund. These days Orsino lived off his own earnings and the trust monies were channelled into charitable programs.

Sure he'd been wild in his youth, not surprising given his family background. But his father made the mistake of thinking he was still eighteen.

Orsino shook his head, his mouth twisting. Who was he kidding?

His decision to make this last climb had been pure defiance, thumbing his nose at his father's manipulations.

Orsino shoved away the covers and sat up, sick of being confined.

He swung his legs over the side of the bed, vowing to be done with emotion. Look where it had got him. Disappointment and, yes, hurt at his father's attitude had sent him on a climb that had been a hairsbreadth from suicidal.

As for Poppy… Orsino paused, pain lancing as he forgot his ribs and took a deep breath.

Poppy made him feel out of control, no longer master of his own destiny. She threatened him in ways his father could never manage.

This vulnerability had to be faced, defeated and destroyed. Then he could get on with his life.

He drew a slow breath and levered himself to his feet, ignoring another sharp throb of pain.

It was time to put his plan into action.

The group of reporters outside the hospital had grown when Poppy returned. Years of practice kept her moving at a steady clip but their shouted questions about a reconciliation with Orsino jarred like physical blows. Every strident call was a lash on tender skin.

Once inside she paused, barely resisting the need to lean against the wall for support.

Reconciliation with Orsino? No way!

He's still your husband, a tiny voice chided.

All at once she felt like the Poppy she'd told herself no

longer existed. The one who'd responded to Orsino's shivery deep voice yesterday as she had all those years ago. The Poppy whose pulse had leapt into a jittering rhythm when he'd touched her. The Poppy who'd been devastated when he'd turned on his heel and left her bereft.

A shudder of unadulterated terror ripped through her.

She wasn't that girl any more.

She'd rebuilt herself into someone stronger. Into the woman she'd wanted to be for as long as she could remember—independent and successful. No man would ever take over her life again. She'd seen that side of the coin with her mother. For an awful time she'd *been* there herself. She wouldn't let herself be so vulnerable again.

Her relationship with Orsino had been an aberration—proof she'd been right in not wanting romantic love.

Love made you weak.

Poppy straightened, her tattered confidence growing.

She could deal with Orsino. Besides, for all his faults and the anger that stirred when she remembered the past, she pitied him those injuries.

Setting her shoulders she knocked and entered Orsino's room. He wasn't there and for one heart-stopping moment Poppy wondered if he'd taken a turn for the worse.

'You're late.'

Hand to chest, she spun around, her heart catapulting.

Orsino sat in a wheelchair, surveying her. The bandages around his eyes were gone, replaced by glasses so black she caught no hint of his eyes behind them.

'Your eyes.' It was more question than statement, but he said nothing, merely sat statue still, facing her.

Was he blind? Infuriatingly he said nothing, shutting her out completely.

Her belly cramped. He was an expert at that.

Most of the bandages on his head had been removed, except for one at a rakish angle that made him look like a stranger. A tough stranger you wouldn't want to mess with.

Yet she'd know the angle of that cheekbone, the strong thrust of his nose and that square jaw even in her sleep.

Poppy told herself it was natural to remember so much. He'd been her first lover, after all.

Though the plan was to leave for France today, it was a shock to see him in street clothes. The image of Orsino buried in bandages had haunted her through the long, sleepless night.

Now a casual jacket hung loose from one shoulder, partly covering his sling, and he wore a pale chambray shirt. Jeans clung to his long, solid thighs. Hiking boots encased his feet on the wheelchair's footrest.

Poppy worked to smother unwilling sympathy.

'They must have cut the sleeve to get that shirt on.' Her voice emerged just right, even and easy.

'Trust a model to consider the clothes first and foremost.' The words were an accusation that sliced straight through her. And the way he said *model* as if it was a euphemism for something ugly...

Her lips firmed as indignation ignited. Did she really want to deal with Orsino in condescending mode?

Being with him was an outrageously bad idea. Every instinct screamed at her to walk away. He could spill his version of their break-up to the press and she'd survive. He could make divorce difficult but he couldn't stop it.

It wasn't too late to back out.

Except she was determined never to reveal vulnerability before him again. If she reneged on the deal he'd know it for weakness.

She had to face him and prove these *feelings* were mere phantoms of memory.

Poppy squared her jaw. She was woman enough to cope with him. After what she'd been through a few jibes were nothing.

'You'd prefer if I made a fuss of you?' She stepped closer, watching for some sign he could see her but his face remained impassive. Deep in her stomach tension swirled at the possibility he couldn't see, and worse, he'd never see again.

She cleared a knot in her throat. 'If you're after someone to simper and sigh over you you've picked the wrong woman. Call one of your girlfriends instead.'

'The claws are out, I see.'

Poppy shrugged, meeting that blank, reflective stare. 'No claws. That implies I have a personal, emotional interest.' She paused to let that sink in. 'The only reason I'm allowing you to impose yourself is the prospect of a gloriously Chatsfield-free future.' Poppy let her mouth curve in a smile that she knew didn't reach her eyes. 'Besides, no matter what you think of me I'm not the sort to kick a man while he's down.'

No matter how much he deserved it.

'So tell me, Orsino, what do the doctors say? I need to know if I'm going to help you.'

The sight of that wheelchair did nothing to dispel her concern. Had he damaged his spine? The idea chilled her to the marrow.

His lips twisted and she sensed his impatience.

'They counsel patience.'

No wonder he was moody. Pain would be bad enough, but for Orsino, waiting to recuperate would be even worse. 'I see.'

'I'm glad someone does.' He spoke under his breath but his bitter tone cut through the still air.

Poppy stepped closer, her gaze on those dark glasses. 'You can't see at all?'

He expelled a breath in a rush of air. 'Let's just say I won't be driving a car any time soon.'

Poppy sucked in a sharp breath. Words of sympathy rose on her tongue but she forced them away, knowing he'd reject them. Instead she aimed for brisk and pragmatic.

'If you're blind, Orsino, I need to know. We're returning to a photo shoot.' She stumbled over 'we're' and had to force down a pang of doubt. 'I'll be working long hours so I'll be on-site but not always at hand. If you can't see you'll need a full-time carer.'

His lips turned up in a smile that showed his teeth. He looked like he wanted to snap a bite out of her.

'God forbid that I should interfere with your exalted career.' His drawl made the hairs on her nape rise and her jaw clench.

She refused to fight that battle again. Orsino had lost the right to an opinion years ago.

Poppy waited till her riotous pulse subsided before answering. 'I refuse to be goaded, Orsino. I understand you're hurting and scared but if you think you can take that out on me you're mistaken.'

She ignored his hiss of indrawn breath. It was about time someone made him face the truth. 'I'm not your whipping boy.' She folded her arms, glaring down at him. 'If you can't understand that then the deal is off. I've already disrupted a very expensive shoot to be here, so don't try your high-and-mighty attitude on me. I don't expect gratitude.' A sour laugh escaped at the very idea. 'But I do expect common courtesy and politeness.'

Orsino leaned forward as if reading her features. 'You've changed,' he said finally. Poppy wasn't sure if that was approval or regret in his voice.

'I should hope so!' She'd been unbearably naive when they'd met. You'd have thought her upbringing would have toughened her up but when it came to Orsino she'd been lamentably innocent. She'd been swept away on a fantasy of love that even common sense couldn't puncture. Until it was too late.

'Common courtesy? I think I can manage that. If you can.'

He shrugged and Poppy watched as those wide shoulders snagged her gaze again. Even in a wheelchair Orsino emanated a concentrated masculinity. It was just as well she was immune to him....

'Good, now perhaps you'll answer my question. Can you see?'

Orsino looked up at the slim woman standing rigid before him. One thing was clear. If he hadn't been able to let the past go completely, nor had she.

Even with his poor vision he saw Poppy was on edge, ramrod stiff, shoulders hunched and arms crossed. He still got under her skin.

But there was more. She also looked gorgeous: sexy and alluring in a bone-deep way that had nothing to do with makeup or lighting. To his chagrin he wasn't impervious.

His gut tightened as dormant parts of his body stirred.

His gaze lingered on the elegant sweep of her throat and jaw. The lush mouth she'd bemoaned wasn't wide enough and he'd always found perfect. The stunning eyes he'd lost himself in time and again when they'd climaxed together.

Something akin to shame flooded him that after all this time he still remembered.

'I can see but not well,' he finally admitted, turning his head away. How much did he see when he looked at Poppy and how much did memory superimpose? Looking towards the window he could make out dark and light, shapes and shadows, but there was none of the clarity with which he'd viewed her.

Damn! How long before he recovered?

'What I see is distorted and I'm sensitive to light. So as I say, I won't be driving for a while.' Orsino shoved aside the fear that perhaps he'd never drive, or climb, or parachute again. He scrubbed his jaw with his unbandaged hand. He'd even needed help shaving!

'I'm sure I'll be able to manage for myself while you're

working.' He was careful not to let doubt enter his voice. He *would* manage, even if it killed him.

His mouth twisted in a mirthless smile. Not so long ago he'd faced the prospect of death head-on. Was that why every moment now was so vivid and emotion so close to the surface?

'And the wheelchair? Will you need that to board the plane?' Poppy's clipped questions scraped away at his pride. He hated being unable to manage for himself.

If he'd expected concern he should have known better. She didn't ask because she cared but so she could work out how little assistance to give.

Orsino told himself that didn't hurt. Hadn't he always managed alone? As kids he and Lucca had been all but abandoned by their parents, given everything money could buy but left to fend for themselves.

His mouth curved derisively. Just as well he'd never learned to expect sympathy. He had as much chance of genuine caring from his wife as a heatwave on Everest.

Had she *ever* cared for him? Or had it all been a clever con to win her money and fame? The question was like a canker inside, eating away at him.

If nothing else, he intended to discover the answer.

'You were imagining the photos, were you? The brave wife wheeling her incapacitated hero?'

Poppy didn't rise to the bait. Just stood silent and unmoving and suddenly the urge to bait her died. Exhaustion tugged at his body, making him slump in the chair.

He sighed. 'I can walk, but given my vision—' and the lacerations and bruising '—I'm not as mobile as I was. The wheelchair is at the insistence of the staff—' who'd continued to badger him about staying. 'I'll use it as far as the entrance but after that I'll walk.' He just hoped he didn't make a fool of himself by collapsing in a heap. Getting ready had sapped more strength than he'd anticipated.

Abruptly Orsino gestured to the wheelchair. He'd had

enough of this conversation. 'Given the sling it's hard to push. Do you mind?'

'Of course.' She hurried behind him and he caught a faint scent of berries on the air. He ignored it.

They had to run the gamut of staff who'd assembled to see him off. At the entrance Orsino carefully stood, his body creaking like an old man's.

'Are you sure you're fit to walk?' It was Amindra, his favourite nurse. Her concern was at odds with her usual brisk kindness and he found himself groping for her hand. This round dumpling of a woman had given him more care and concern than he remembered from his own mother.

Had Poppy really been jealous of her?

'Of course I am, Amindra. Thanks to your care. When I'm healed I'll be back to thank you all properly.'

He thought he caught a glimpse of a smile before she curled his hands around the head of a walking stick.

'Good. Then you can bring this back to me.' She squeezed his hand then melted into the gloom that was his peripheral vision.

'This way.' It was Poppy, beside him again, her voice as colourless as a mountain brook. She swept one arm in a wide gesture and he located the door.

Slowly he paced beside her, his good hand clenched around the walking stick, his body tense with effort.

The big door swung open with a whoosh of crisp air. He hesitated then stepped out, relishing the cocktail of smells bombarding him: exhaust fumes and dust, smoke and spicy cooking. It was so different to the scoured smell of the hospital. He heard bustling life surround him. Relief battered like a wave, making him light-headed.

Not even to himself had he admitted to fear that he'd never leave the hospital. Yet he felt a weight slide off his shoulders.

'Orsino! Orsino! Over here!'

He blinked, trying and failing to focus on the faces surrounding him. His heart drummed in his chest and a cold sweat broke out on his brow. Something suspiciously like panic twisted in his gut.

A hand closed around his sleeve.

Poppy. She was there beside him.

He breathed deep, hating the way tension eased because he wasn't alone. Hating the fact that she felt the way his arm shook. *She* of all women.

It was one thing to imagine her pandering to his every whim while he regained his strength. It was another to have her guess how much this cost him. To know how much he needed her right now. His pride smarted.

Gritting his teeth, Orsino walked on, aware of the warmth of her hand through the sleeve of his jacket. Aware, too, of the curious leap of excitement he felt being close to her again.

As they walked slowly the voices grew strident and blurred faces crowded close.

'Can you see, Orsino?'

'How close did you come to death?'

'Are you and Poppy reconciling? Are you in love after all this time? How about a kiss for the camera?'

Poppy spoke. 'The car is straight ahead.' There was nothing in her tone, neither stress nor sympathy. She might have been talking to a stranger.

He hadn't expected her to feel anything. He'd had her measure since the night five years ago when he'd discovered what she really was.

Why did it matter that he'd been mistaken in the hospital, imagining he'd got under her skin? Why did it matter that he meant nothing to her?

Yet it did.

Because almost dying out there on the mountain, he'd faced the terrible truth that some part of him was still connected to her.

The realisation was like salt poured on an open wound. A

wound he'd believed healed. His gut churned with the force of his reaction as years of resentment came flooding free.

Someone jostled them and his stick clattered to the ground. He reached out and found himself grasping soft cashmere and even softer hair. His fingers tightened.

'That's it, Orsino. Just one kiss!' Around them the paparazzi pressed closer.

'Can you stand while I reach for your stick?' Poppy's words were innocent enough but her ice-cool tone struck him again. To her he was an encumbrance till the divorce, a necessary responsibility. No more.

Five years ago she'd made a fool of him. Even now, when he'd blackmailed her into dancing to his tune, he hadn't dented her self-assurance, much less her emotions.

Impotent fury spiked.

He *would* get a reaction from her.

Planting his feet more solidly, he released his hold and heard her breath sigh out. But before she could draw away he lifted his hand to the back of her head, to the silk tresses that moved as she jerked beneath his hold.

Her tangy, sweet scent filled his nostrils.

'Orsino?' Her voice wobbled.

Now *that* was a reaction.

He looked down into wide eyes. The fiery burn in his belly flared and spread as he held her tight and slanted his mouth over hers.

CHAPTER FOUR

POPPY COULD HAVE broken away from him. She *should*. He held her with one arm only, the plaster on his other arm pressing against her middle.

His splayed hand held her firmly but not unbreakably.

So why did she hesitate as his mouth captured hers?

Maybe it was the surprising restraint in the touch of his cool lips against hers. It reminded her of the first time they'd kissed. Then he'd scooped her close, his shoulders blocking out the world, leaving her cocooned in the passion that swirled like a maelstrom between them. Yet he'd taken her mouth with a gentleness that had been more devastating than any urgent caress. He'd undone her with one simple kiss, because she'd felt not only desired but cherished.

His mouth moved now against hers, pressing gently. Poppy felt the years peel back, as if awakening to a man for the first time.

A shudder ran the length of her body as nerve endings sprang to life.

His tongue swept the seam of her lips, coaxing a response that rippled through her, from her mouth down to her tingling nipples and her toes curling in her boots.

Orsino's hand moved in her hair, long fingers strong and hard and ridiculously erotic given all he did was hold her.

Her heart hammered into her breastbone and her eyes fluttered shut as her lips moved tentatively against his.

Sensation flooded her, the sound of blood pulsing in

her ears, the tensile strength of him against her, the dark chocolate and spice deliciousness that was the shockingly familiar taste of Orsino on her tongue.

He pressed closer and reason finally surfaced from the inchoate thoughts tumbling through her mind.

She pulled back, eyes wide at her body's betrayal.

Impenetrable dark glasses stared back at her. Her eyes dropped to the thin, mobile mouth that had so easily worked magic on hers. She caught a gleam of dampness on his bottom lip, the sheen where her mouth had met his.

Wrenching free of his hold, Poppy staggered back, heart pounding, her breath sawing from her lips.

Still he stood unmoving while all around them cameras clicked and whirred and reporters climbed over one another for a better view.

She felt like she'd had an out of body experience. It sure wasn't her body that had responded to Orsino so eagerly. It couldn't be. She'd eradicated him from her system.

Pity your body doesn't know it.

The snide little voice came from inside her head.

Imagine what would have happened if he'd had two hands to work with.

Poppy wanted to clap her palms over her ears but there was no escaping the truth.

Not even the paparazzi cameras had saved her from herself. The truth punched hard into her empty stomach.

Orsino had laid his mouth on hers and she'd not only let him, but kissed him back. As if she were ripe for the plucking, just waiting for him to offer her a taste of the physical pleasure that had always been his specialty.

As if what he'd done meant nothing.

As if she were just another woman eager to be noticed by the sexy, charismatic Orsino Chatsfield.

Hadn't she learned *anything*?

Even if her body responded to some echo of past attraction, surely she had more sense than to follow in her mother's footsteps, unable to break away from a man who was no good for her.

The thought brought a ball of searing bile to her throat. She gagged and swallowed, ashamed of herself.

Swiftly she scooped up Orsino's walking stick, ignoring the jostling reporters and their raucous questions. Despite their noise it felt as if she and Orsino were closed off from them, caught in a fragile bubble. She couldn't read his features. Was he as impassive as he looked? What about the convulsive way his hand had clamped her skull?

'Here.' She thrust the stick into his grip then shoved her hands into her pockets. He could manage without her.

Poppy pushed aside the memory of his tension as he'd walked beside her. He'd been shaking, muscles bunched and rigid. She'd been foolish enough to feel sorry for him, reading the stress in his tight jaw and pale face.

No more!

She wasn't her mother to be swayed so easily by sympathy for a man who despised her.

She wasn't that self-destructive.

'The car is just a couple of metres away.' She turned and pushed her way through the throng.

They were silent on the way to the airport. Twice Poppy opened her mouth to give Orsino an indignant blast and twice she caught the driver sneaking a peek at them in the rear-view mirror and looked away.

That kiss would be all over the press. The last thing she needed was an eyewitness account of her and Orsino arguing.

Restlessly she pulled the tie from her hair, scooped back the stray curls that had escaped and twisted the mass high on her head, tugging so tight she winced.

Good. A bit of pain might knock some sense into her. What had she been thinking, letting Orsino kiss her?

There was a jittery, excited feeling in her stomach. Horror, she assured herself, not excitement.

She shifted in her seat, unable to repress the shivers tightening her skin.

Finally they arrived at the airport, but instead of drawing up at the terminal, the car went to a private entrance. They passed security staff and drove onto the tarmac where a sleek jet stood, its door open and staff waiting at the bottom of the stairs.

'A private jet? That's how you travel now?'

'Not usually. But it seemed most convenient in the circumstances.' A quick gesture encompassed his glasses and plastered arm. He sounded perfectly composed. No roiling stomach for Orsino after that scene in front of the paparazzi. No regrets or concerns.

Poppy's fingers curled till the nails bit her palms. She wished she could be so blasé.

'The hotel business must be booming.' She shoved open her door and swung her legs out.

'I'm not in the hotel business.'

Something in his voice made her turn in time to see him flatten his lips as if in distaste.

Poppy tilted her head, watching his long fingers flex then clench into a fist. She frowned. Orsino was so good at guarding his thoughts. Did he realise the tension he was signalling?

'I know you don't have to work for a crust, Orsino.' Carefully she kept her voice neutral. His attitude to her career had never been supportive, as if he couldn't understand her need to pay her own way. 'But your family fortune comes from hotels. It's the same thing.'

He opened his mouth as if to say something then paused. 'The jet belongs to a friend,' he said at last.

Poppy hesitated, about to call him on his blatant change of subject then shrugged. She wasn't interested in what made Orsino tick. He'd cured her of caring.

Twenty minutes later they were finally alone, seated on opposite sides of the cabin. The plane had lifted off and the steward had retired to the galley after serving drinks.

'What the hell did you think you were doing back there, Orsino?' Her outrage hadn't abated. Her fingers were white-knuckled around her glass.

'Where?' He turned his head towards her but his expression was unreadable behind those glasses.

'Oh, don't be so coy.' She all but grated her teeth together. 'Outside the hospital.'

'What? The kiss?'

'Of course, the kiss.' Heat saturated her skin at the nerve of the man pretending not to understand. 'What did you think gave you the right to do that?'

Above the dark glasses one black eyebrow arched. 'A husband's right?' he purred in a whisky-deep voice.

'A husband's—!' Her words were cut off as she surged upwards, only to find herself restrained by the seatbelt. With a fumbled click she freed herself and shot to her feet, stalking across the luxurious lounge to stand before him. She shook with the force of her indignation.

'How many times do we have to go through this, Orsino? You're no longer my husband.'

Slowly, oh so slowly, he lifted his head towards her voice. Her skin prickled as his gaze trawled her body, from her hips, past her waist to her breasts and then finally to her face. Heat surged in her cheeks.

Could he see her or was he just pretending, yanking her chain? Either way, his leisurely survey set her teeth on edge, like fingernails scraping down a chalkboard.

Poppy wrapped her arms around herself rather than reach out to wrap her hands around his throat. She'd never in her life been violent but Orsino brought out a response more potent than any she'd known.

Except the depth of misery and hurt he'd left in his wake. The memory of that helped get her anger under control.

'You didn't like kissing me?' He tilted his head as if puzzled. But the shadow of a smile lurking at the corner of his mouth told its own story. 'You could have fooled me.'

Poppy swung away, pacing the deep, plush carpet. 'Then obviously I succeeded. Being kissed by you isn't an experience I want to repeat. Ever. I prefer to save my kisses for someone I care about.'

Silence.

'And does this man have a name? Or can I guess?' Orsino's voice held a dangerous edge, like honed steel sheathed in velvet. It abraded her senses, making her shiver.

'That falls in the category of none of your business.' He had a hide, prying into her private life after all this time.

Orsino's lips twisted up in a smile she could only describe as feral. 'If you try to flaunt him under my nose while we're together you'll find it's very much my business.'

Poppy spun around to stare at him. Reflective glasses met her gaze, giving nothing away.

'Now hold on right there. We're not *together*. I'm letting you stay for a few weeks. What I do and who I see is nothing to do with you, Orsino.'

'Perhaps not.' He lifted his glass and took a slow sip. 'But I think you'll discover, dear Poppy, that the press will make it their business to ferret out the juicy details of this man you care for so much. Imagine the fallout when news breaks of your affair even as you're nursing your poor, wounded husband.'

'You… You…!'

'I'm just telling it like it is. You know what the paparazzi are like.' He paused. 'Will I meet him? Is he at this shoot you're taking me to?'

Poppy darted a disbelieving glance at Orsino, casually sipping his drink. Did he think he could just ask and she'd open up?

She shook her head. The man was amazing.

'You seem inordinately interested in my love life.'

He said nothing but his lips tightened. Poppy frowned. Why would he take an interest? He hadn't for five long years.

The memory of her unanswered calls and emails stiffened her spine. She didn't trust his sudden fascination with her personal life.

'What are you up to, Orsino? Are you trying to make it look like we're reconciling? Is that why you kissed me?' Though what he had to gain she had no idea.

'You put too much weight on an innocent kiss.'

It was on the tip of Poppy's tongue to say that for all his restraint there'd been nothing innocent about that kiss. It had been pure temptation, designed to make a woman melt.

She rubbed her hands up her arms, dispelling the goosebumps that rose when she thought about it.

'You haven't answered my question. What were you hoping to achieve?' She crossed the space to stand before him. Light from the window shafted across his face, throwing the grooves around his mouth into shadow. They gave his face a sardonic cast.

'Who says I have an agenda?' He tilted his head and she was sure his eyes met hers from behind those black glasses. She felt the sizzle of his regard right to her toes. 'It was a spur-of-the-moment thing. An impulse.'

Her eyebrows rose in disbelief.

'An impulse? With the press on hand? You're kidding.'

He waved his glass expansively. 'I fail to see the problem. It was just a friendly kiss. No harm done. Besides, you thrive on press attention. That should keep the pundits busy for a couple of days.' His lips curled in a smile she didn't trust. 'Consider it a gift from me. Some free publicity.'

'Free publicity! As if I need that.' She drew herself up and glared at him.

She'd learned how intrusive the press could be. The year after their separation had been sheer torment as the press hounded her for a reaction, any reaction, to their split, to Orsino's latest daredevil stunt and to his string of voluptuously glamorous girlfriends. They'd stalked her, harassed her friends and even gone through her rubbish for stories to print. When they found nothing they just made it up.

'But it's so good for your career, Poppy.' Orsino adopted an unmistakeable accent, a cruel but accurate mimicry she had no trouble recognising.

Her fingers bit into her arms as she hugged herself tight. Her jaw ached from the control she exerted.

Thank heaven Mischa wasn't staying at the chateau. She didn't like to think what would happen if the pair crossed paths again. Her stomach churned and nausea rose.

How had she agreed to this absurd idea? What was she trying to prove to herself?

That you're free of him, remember? That there's no tiny part of you still hankering for what might have been.

'It may have escaped your notice, but I'm a highly sought-after model. One of the best. I don't need to court public attention. I succeed on my own merits.'

Orsino remained silent as he swirled the liquid in his glass, the ice tinkling softly in the silence. It was a silence that said more than she needed to know about his views on her success.

She'd worked incredibly hard to get where she was. She deserved a little respect. But Orsino had never respected her career, had he? It was one of the many things that had come between them.

Poppy strode across the cabin and braced her hands either side of a window. Below them a mass of white cloud obscured the land. They were stuck together, alone. Claustrophobia grabbed her by the throat. She felt trapped, exposed and there was no way out.

'Don't tell me you had no idea of the furore you've stirred up. It's bad enough they saw us leaving together but this…' She shook her head. Now it would start all over again.

She swung around to see him leaning towards her, his half-full glass on the table.

'What did you hope to gain, Orsino? Or were you just stirring the pot?'

'Maybe I was simply curious.' His deep voice swirled softly around her. 'It's been a long time.'

Shock held her motionless while she took in his predatory stillness. The air thickening to a sultry heat.

Then he reached up and removed his glasses. Dark eyes held hers, the intensity of his stare like the touch of a hand on her face.

Poppy tried to tell herself it was the look of a man straining to bring her into focus through damaged eyes. But her heart thumped as their gazes locked. Heat shimmied through her insides. It must be shock at the sight of the angry scar running from beneath the remaining bandage and down so close to his eye.

'Well, now that you've satisfied your curiosity, you can keep your hands to yourself.'

Slowly his mouth turned up into a smile. This time it was genuine. She saw it in his eyes.

Poppy sucked in a startled breath. Even with the bandage and the scar, it transformed him into the man she'd once fallen in love with.

Her pulse gave a tremulous flutter then took off at a gallop.

'There's only one complication.' He paused as if to let his words sink in. 'That wasn't a kiss, not a proper one. It was more like a taste.' He shook his head, his eyes brimful of devilry. 'It would take a *proper* kiss to satisfy my curiosity.'

'How very inconvenient for you.' Poppy forced herself to stroll past him, the picture of nonchalance, and subside onto a leather armchair on the other side of the cabin. She reached for a glossy magazine and opened it. 'That's the last kiss, proper or not, you'll ever get from me.'

Orsino stretched stiff legs. He should rest on the king-size bed in the plane's suite. He ached all over and his head throbbed with a gentle pulse of pain. If Amindra were here she'd fuss over him with that motherly brusqueness he'd found so unaccountably appealing.

He rubbed his jaw, feeling the scratch on his palm.

He'd overestimated his strength in leaving the hospital. His mouth turned down. His pride had almost resulted in a fall when he'd lost the walking stick. Luckily Poppy had been there to save him.

Poppy. He turned to where she slumped in the massive armchair, the magazine she'd been reading on the floor at her feet as she slept. A skein of wavy dark hair trailed tantalisingly down over her shoulder.

That's the last kiss, proper or not, you'll ever get from me.

She hadn't even looked at him when she said it, as if his presence didn't disturb her in the least.

That was bad enough. Even worse was the fact all he could think of was stealing a kiss from her that was improper in every way. A kiss that would lead to hot, hungry, raunchy sex. Sex with a kick to it.

Hell!

He scraped his hand over his face.

A week ago he'd thought himself dying. A couple of days ago he'd felt exposed, exhausted, *mortal* in a way he never had before. It wasn't till you faced death head-on that you valued life as you should.

Now he was weary, bleary-eyed, fighting to keep control of a body that wanted to hibernate till the pain passed, yet his libido had roared into full-blooded life.

One taste of Poppy did that.

Orsino shut his eyes, cursing under his breath.

How could he be so needy?

How could he want her again, knowing what she was?

Talk about being hoist with his own petard! He'd brought this on himself.

He'd planned to exact a little revenge and in the process

assure himself she was out of his system for good. Instead he discovered he craved her as strongly as he had when their marriage meant something.

Then he'd never been able to get enough of her.

Orsino tried to tell himself this was the predictable result of sexual abstinence but it didn't work. He'd merely touched Poppy's lips, clamped his hand in her hair and she'd undone him.

What would it be like to kiss her properly? To lose himself in the hot warmth of her mouth, let his hands loose on that svelte body he knew was strong and supple and indescribably sexy. A body that came alive like kindling to flame at his touch.

Would it still?

His breath hitched as he imagined Poppy aroused and needy, begging him for release. Her hands boldly stroking, her mouth poutingly soft and inviting.

He rubbed a hand around the back of his neck, as if he could rub away the prickle of heat building there. Self-disgust filled him. He should be able to turn his back on her as easily as if she didn't exist.

Except turning his back on Poppy had never been easy, even when it had been a matter of survival.

Orsino grimaced. His body was telling him something so obvious he couldn't avoid it any longer.

How long since he'd been aroused by the mere touch of a woman? How long since he'd wanted one like this?

For too long he'd sublimated desire because it reminded him of his weakness for Poppy Graham. Because inevitably they were her dark violet eyes that swam in his brain when arousal stirred, her throaty mews of pleasure he heard when he woke from an erotic dream.

He'd told himself he'd left her behind the night he walked out of their London apartment, but he'd been mistaken. Buried in ice and rock, facing his own extinction, he'd realised there was still something between them. And now he knew what it was.

Sex. Animal attraction. Desire.

Orsino wanted her as he hadn't wanted in so long it didn't bear thinking about.

His good hand gripped the leather chair, fingers digging in as if to anchor himself.

Logic said it was an illusion. The reality of being intimate with the woman who'd smashed his life asunder couldn't be anything like his imaginings. It wasn't as if he cared for her any more. She'd made sure of that.

But there was no denying she heated his blood. Just parading in front of him with her hip-swaying stroll had brought him out in a sweat.

What to do about it?

He wanted to obliterate her from his life and kill that niggling sense of unfinished business between them.

He also wanted her with an urgency that shouldn't be possible in a body so battered.

Orsino smiled. He'd always been tough. 'Indestructible,' the press had dubbed him.

The smile faded as he surveyed his companion. There was one obvious option. Sleep with Poppy and let disappointing reality destroy the fantasy of her he still harboured. He knew she was poison. But the part of him that knew good sex had him hankering after a woman he shouldn't want to touch with a barge pole.

Sleep with her and destroy that last subliminal craving. His smile returned. It had the advantage of being exactly what he wanted to do.

A few weeks holed up at this chateau where she was working. Plenty of time to seduce her and free himself before he walked away for good.

How could he resist?

CHAPTER FIVE

IT WAS CRISP early morning as the limousine slowed to enter the quaint French town. Beside her, Orsino stirred at last, stretching his long legs.

He looked fresher than she felt. Clearly he'd slept on the flight far better than she with her restless dreams. He'd emerged from the plane's bedroom freshly shaven and in a crisp new shirt, thanks to the steward.

Orsino looked casually sexy but with that dangerous edge advertisers the world over paid a fortune for. He would have made a brilliant model with his handsome features and raw masculinity. Only the tight grooves beside his mouth hinted at discomfort.

It wasn't fair. Even bandaged he looked terrific while she felt rumpled and untidy.

Poppy straightened, pinning back the strands of hair that always managed to escape.

'Who organised all this?' Her gesture took in the car and driver. 'I'd planned to hire a car from the airport.' She thought guiltily of her relief when she'd discovered the car waiting for them. At the time she'd accepted it with weary relief, but on the drive she'd had time to ponder. She couldn't imagine Orsino making the necessary calls from his hospital bed.

'My secretary.'

'You have a secretary?' She didn't hide her surprise. 'You

used to manage your social calendar without help. Surely it's not that demanding.'

He turned to survey her and Poppy wished he'd ditch the glasses. Shocking as it had been to meet the blaze of his knowing eyes, it had been better than wondering what was hidden behind the dark shades.

'She does more than organise my social calendar.' His tone was smooth and almost expressionless. Almost.

'Oh, yes? What else?'

He'd jealously guarded his expeditions, even the planning of them, from her. She'd felt excluded—more evidence that whatever his reasons for marrying her, it wasn't to share his life.

Could it be he'd finally let someone into that part of his world? The notion jabbed pain between her ribs and she stiffened.

Poppy blinked and tore her gaze away. She couldn't be *jealous* of his secretary! Yet she couldn't suppress her curiosity. What did this secretary look like?

'I suppose those expeditions of yours take some organising now.' They'd grown more dangerous and more public, but she didn't mention that. She didn't want him to think she'd been following him in the media. 'Does she work part-time?'

'Full-time, though she tells me she's long overdue for a vacation.'

'Really?' Poppy frowned. Surely even setting up arrangements for Orsino's high-profile expeditions wasn't a full-time job twelve months a year. She turned back to him, the set of his mouth hinting there was something else he hadn't said. 'But surely—'

'I take it this is our destination?' Orsino nodded towards the window and Poppy recognised the tall gates barring the chateau from the public.

A guard stepped forward and she wound down her window to greet him. Instantly he grinned, welcoming her effusively. Moments later the gates slid silently open.

'Another of your many admirers?' Orsino's dark voice held a steely edge.

Poppy gritted her teeth and reminded herself there was no point rising to the bait.

'I have to work today.' She'd already checked her messages and knew she had a full schedule. 'But I'll get you settled first.'

'Sounds good. I'm looking forward to having you put me to bed and tuck me in.'

She turned from the avenue of arching plane trees to stare at Orsino. His tone implied something far too intimate. The way he sprawled in his corner of the seat, a complacent smile hovering at the corner of his mouth, made her stiffen. She opened her mouth then snapped it shut.

Deliberately she looked away.

The car crunched up the long driveway, out into the open between lawns, passing the converted stables and farm buildings on the right, heading straight for the chateau. It rose out of the river mist like something from a fairytale. Pale stone, round towers and surprisingly large windows. More palace than fortress.

It stood framed by the deep russet of the late-autumn forest on the far bank, like a pearl against crimson velvet. From here you couldn't see the length of the building, stretching back over the river on a series of arched supports.

Poppy couldn't prevent a smile. She loved this place, its romance, the delicacy and beauty of it. Its tranquillity was a balm after her hectic schedule.

The car pulled up beside the round, free-standing tower a couple of hundred metres before the chateau. With its conical roof it looked like a setting for Rapunzel.

'I'll say this. Whoever chose the setting for your commercial knew what they were doing.'

Poppy's smile disappeared, her heart dipping. Orsino's

reaction would be completely different if he knew who'd organised this series of commercials.

Even she'd had doubts about the job. Not for professional reasons—it promised to be a huge success—but for purely personal ones. Ever since that night in London, Poppy hadn't been able to work with Mischa. But she'd finally convinced herself it was time to let the past go. Besides, the income from this contract would give her the financial security that had been her goal for so long. She'd be a fool to pass up the opportunity.

And, as she kept telling herself, the past was the past.

'Poppy?' Orsino's voice dragged her into the present.

'I'm glad you approve.' She pushed open her door, not waiting for the chauffeur. The air was brisk and she shivered, telling herself the prickle up her back wasn't a premonition of disaster.

All too soon they and their luggage were inside, the driver gone.

It was ridiculous to feel nervous, but Poppy was as edgy as a cat on hot sand.

For the first time in five years she and Orsino were completely alone. At the hospital and on the plane there had always been the possibility of staff appearing. But here, in the luxuriously fitted tower, a completely separate building to the chateau and the other accommodation on the vast estate, there was just the two of them.

A low whistle pierced the stillness. 'This is really something.'

Orsino moved to an open door leading to the beautiful sitting room that looked over the formal rose garden and the river. He leaned on his stick, staring first at the view then the priceless renaissance paintwork on the high ceiling beams and down to the dark honey parquetry floor with its intricate weave pattern.

'If it wasn't so crass I'd ask who you had to sleep with to get this place to yourself.'

Instantly the chill at Poppy's spine turned to a shaft of ice that twisted and pierced her chest. She swayed at the casual cruelty of the comment, but by the time he turned around she had herself in hand. She stood tall and proud, pretending that poisoned dart hadn't hit its target. Yet she felt brittle, as if one touch would make her shatter.

'No one, as it happens.' Her voice was as crisp as the late-autumn chill. 'It's one of the perks of being the new face of Europe's oldest and premier jewellery house.' Poppy pinned on a smile even though it felt like her facial muscles cracked from the strain. 'The House of Baudin takes care of its assets.'

'I didn't mean—'

'Don't!' She stopped him with a single slashing gesture. To her surprise it worked and he stood silent.

'Of course you meant it. You've got a cutting tongue, Orsino, and your readiness to think the worst is one of your more obvious and less endearing qualities.'

She stopped and heaved in a breath as adrenaline surged, making her quiver with the effort of standing to face him. With that one remark he'd sliced right to the core of her pain, opening up the past like a cleaver cutting to bone.

Her chest rose and fell and she worked to calm herself.

'I did *not* sleep my way to the top of my profession. I got where I am through hard work and dedication. That's *all*. And if you think to smear my reputation—'

Orsino raised his hand. 'I spoke without thinking.'

As if she'd believe that.

Why had she agreed to have him here? Already she'd had more than enough.

'I didn't think you'd be so sensitive. After all, it's a common expression.'

Sensitive! He had the nerve.

'You think I'm such a tart I wouldn't object to your assumption?' Her hands found her hips as she stepped into his personal space.

Instantly he paced forward to meet her, his jaw jutting. The air between them sizzled with tension. His heat and his masculine scent enveloped her. They were so close his sling grazed her jacket but she stood her ground.

Something eddied in her belly. She told herself it was distaste.

'You're the one who slept around, Poppy. Not me.' He bit the words out in sharp chunks and her head snapped back as if from a slap.

The gloves were off.

'Or are you going to try to convince me you went to bed with him and nothing happened? That you're an innocent?' Orsino's voice vibrated with the force of his accusation.

Familiar nausea swamped her. It was like reliving those nightmares that had haunted her since that night in London. In those, no matter what she said, no matter what she did, it all went wrong, over and over and over again. Just as it had gone wrong all those years before when Orsino had refused to hear her out.

She remembered her pain and disbelief then, her anguish when Orsino hadn't let her talk. Her unanswered phone calls and emails. The fruitless attempts to locate him in person. She'd tried and tried to get through to him, but he'd been intractable, uncaring of her fragile state. And through it all the press, intrusive and inquisitive, pestering her for more, snapping photos and revealing her pain to the world.

Dragging herself through those black days of grief, despair and disbelief had been the hardest thing she'd ever done. For a while she'd thought herself fatally wounded. That she'd never recover.

Her eyes narrowed on the dark glasses less than an arm's length away. It wasn't her fault he didn't know the truth. He hadn't *wanted* to know. And she didn't care any more.

Deliberately she tossed her head back. 'Convince you I was innocent? I wouldn't waste my breath.'

Already she'd spent too long trying to do exactly that.

Why bother now? What she'd thought they'd shared had been an illusion.

Besides, there was no way she could convince him of the truth now. He'd judged her guilty then. His attitude now confirmed nothing had changed.

Vertical lines furrowed his brow and Poppy felt a moment's triumph that at least she hadn't been as predictable as he expected. Had he wanted her to plead and grovel? Her days of doing that were over. Orsino didn't want to know the truth. He'd made up his mind that night before he'd even confronted her.

'Why should I? I have no interest in your forgiveness, Orsino, or in trying to pick up the pieces.'

How could you reassemble something that hadn't been broken but pulverised into dust? She tasted it now, like ashes on her tongue, and grimaced.

'Think what you like, by all means. But keep your thoughts to yourself. If I hear you so much as breathe a comment about my love life you're out of here, deal or no deal.'

Orsino surveyed the disdainful woman who stared him down as if he wasn't half a head taller than her. Even with his damaged vision she was remarkable.

Her pale skin flushed, colour washing those slanted cheekbones, accentuating the elegance of her spare features. Her violet eyes blazed and her lips were lusciously dark where she'd bitten them in her fury.

She was like a defiant queen at the head of an army. He'd never seen her so sexy.

He felt the blood pound, his muscles tightening, testosterone surging. Despite his maimed state he knew the rapacious impulse of a marauding warrior. He wanted to reach out and take her, conquer that feminine hauteur and make her his.

The need for her was a primitive pulse in his belly. His

hand clenched on his cane as he forced himself to stand his ground.

He inhaled through his nose, sucking in the rich, berry scent of her skin.

Mad. He must be mad. She all but flaunted her infidelity in his face and he was turned on!

Orsino had regretted his thoughtless words as soon as they were out. Reminding her of her faithlessness was no way to get into her bed. What about his plan to seduce her?

Excitement throbbed through his body as he watched her struggle to hide the way she panted for breath.

Maybe seduction wasn't the way. Maybe he could infuriate her so much, rouse her animal instincts, that she'd take it out on him physically. He'd gladly weather her nails on his skin for the pleasure of sex with Poppy when she was like this. Urgent, angry, hate-you sex would be amazing with this woman.

He shook his head.

He couldn't believe what he was thinking.

Orsino cleared his throat. 'I apologise. I didn't speak intentionally.'

She shifted as if getting ready to defend herself.

'And believe me, I have no intention of discussing your sex life with anyone.' That was something he intended to be between the two of them. He watched her fury fade. 'Now we've covered that—' he used the firm tone that worked so well when chairing difficult meetings '—I suggest we move on.'

Her eyes widened and her mouth sagged. For a perilous instant Orsino hovered on the brink of leaning across to taste her mouth again.

He gestured to the foyer and the ancient stone staircase. 'Perhaps you'd show me my room so I can settle in.'

Poppy said nothing but after subjecting him to a long stare turned and scooped up one of the bags the chauffeur had delivered. She headed up the stairs without a backward glance.

Orsino stood at the bottom, watching her pale trousers tighten over her buttocks with each step. Slim and toned, his wife was nevertheless rounded in the right places, not abundantly voluptuous but sexy and all woman.

His wife.

Did he really intend to go through with this? After all the lacerating pain she'd inflicted?

Of course he did.

Orsino lived for challenge, for the rush of the next dangerous adventure. How could he turn his back on the prospect of bedding and besting the one woman who'd ever managed to hurt him? He felt more alive when he was with her than scaling the most insurmountable peak.

The realisation punched the air from his lungs.

All these years of thrill seeking and none had surpassed the raw, vibrant adrenaline rush of sparring with Poppy.

Orsino dragged in a rough breath, feeling his battered ribs protest. A shiver rippled through him as he digested the revelation. This game was more dangerous than he'd anticipated.

But since when had he turned his back on danger?

Deliberately he crossed the foyer and, grasping the curved handrail, began to climb the ancient stone steps. It was harder than he liked. His injured side pulsed with the effort.

He gritted his teeth. The sooner he started using his body, the sooner it would mend.

By the time he was halfway up he was sweating, his hand clammy on the railing.

'Here, let me help.'

It was Poppy, coming down to support him. Despite the tight set of her lips, was that concern wrinkling her brow?

'Sure you wouldn't rather push me down the stairs?'

'Don't give me ideas, Orsino. You don't know how tempting that is.' Her mouth twitched and he wondered if she was repressing a smile or the urge to lambast him. 'You need to be in bed. What the hospital was doing releasing you in this state, I don't know.'

'I insisted,' he managed between gritted teeth. He felt ridiculously done in by a simple flight of stairs. 'Those four walls were driving me crazy.'

'Why doesn't that surprise me?' She had her arm around him, her breast soft against his side. Orsino dragged in a quick breath and tried to focus.

Finally they reached the floor and she led him across the landing.

They moved into a vast, almost circular room, dominated by a wide, velvet-covered bed and a series of windows showing different aspects of the formal gardens and river. Once inside Poppy stepped away.

'I hope you're not going to have a relapse. You'll be alone here while I'm working.'

'Not completely. I'll have a health visitor later today.'

'You will?' Her eyebrows rose. 'I didn't think the hospital could organise that in another country.'

Orsino shook his head and eased himself into a stately wing chair, his body sighing with relief. 'Not the hospital but my secretary. The one you doubted actually existed. She's also arranged for me to meet another eye specialist here in France. Very efficient, she is.'

'Obviously.' Poppy peeled back the quilt from the bed and picked up a folded sheet from a nearby chair, lifting it high and snapping it out over the bed. 'I assume she was responsible for the new luggage waiting for you when we touched down.'

'A man has his needs and she's excellent at anticipating them.' He thought of the laptop stacked with the rest of the luggage downstairs and told himself there'd be time for that later. His appalling weakness at merely climbing a staircase troubled him.

'She sounds like a paragon. I take it she's used to working miracles anywhere around the globe.'

'Naturally.'

'She must be quite a woman.' Poppy's voice was clipped, almost disapproving. Did she think his secretary looked after his more *personal* needs? The idea intrigued.

Orsino watched her swift, decisive movements, smoothing the sheet with a brisk arc of her hand. No doubt she wished she could wipe him out of her life as easily as she cleared the wrinkles in the cotton.

'Oh, she is that. Quite amazing.'

Poppy stiffened, shooting him a darting glance, and he suppressed a smile. No doubt about it, despite her anger, his wife was more than a little interested in his relationship with his secretary. He had no intention of letting on that Bettina was a sixty-year-old, wheelchair-bound grandmother. Let Poppy assume he had a sexpot catering to his every whim.

Sitting back, he enjoyed the view as Poppy stretched and bent, making the bed. Supple as ever, her body was slender but strong. His body's dull aches retreated as he let himself imagine her naked on those crisp sheets.

'Is this your bed?'

She stiffened then walked around to the other side, moving with a graceful economy of movement.

'Hardly. I'm on the next floor.'

That settled it. The sooner he conquered those stairs, the better. He needed to be fully mobile.

'Did you say something?' She regarded him suspiciously.

He shook his head and favoured her with a smile. Instantly she froze.

'Before you go, I'd appreciate some help with this shirt and jacket.'

'You want to get changed?' She tucked in the last corner and walked towards him.

'I want to get naked.'

Did the colour washing her cheeks darken?

'You know that's how I always sleep.' He let his voice drop low, watching her reaction. 'If you'll just help me with the sling…'

Poppy surveyed Orsino's easy smile, suspicion rippling across her skin like a rising tide. What was he up to? His scathing comment downstairs had ripped open past wounds and now he played the charm card. Did he think she was some susceptible fool?

But he needed help. That's why she'd gone to him on the stairs. She couldn't leave him swaying there in danger of falling.

'What do you need?'

'Just a hand with these clothes.' He stood and suddenly she was conscious of how quiet it was here, the two of them alone in the luxurious tower bedroom.

Jerkily she nodded. She didn't want to touch Orsino but nor did she want him realising how uncomfortable she was. Ever since seeing him again her reactions had been intense and unpredictable.

'Of course.' She schooled her face into an expressionless mask. Years of work in front of a camera came to her aid.

Scooping off his jacket, she laid it over the arm of the chair. He was already fumbling at his shirt button.

'Here. I'll do that.' She'd be faster, which meant she'd be out of here sooner.

His hand dropped and she reached out, cautious of his sling, and flicked open a button then another. She breathed in then wished she hadn't as her nostrils filled with the cedar wood and spice scent that was uniquely Orsino. No other man had ever smelled as good as he.

Poppy moved lower, trying to ignore his intense heat, once so familiar to her, and the hard-packed muscle just beneath the pristine shirt.

He moved his damaged arm out to give her better access and she sidled around it so her arms were between the sling and his body. Heat trickled between her breasts and they seemed to swell with her quickened breathing. Stupid to feel enclosed by Orsino. He stood passive.

Poppy darted a look at his face but it was impossible to read his expression.

'Do you need the glasses on inside?'

'My eyes are sensitive to light.'

Tentatively she pulled his shirt up and free of his trousers. She hated that her hands trembled. She blinked and shoved aside dim memories of hauling Orsino's shirt free as they made frantic, passionate love.

'There.' She stepped back, surveying him. Then her heart sank as she realised she wasn't done yet. He couldn't get the shirt off without her.

Touching Orsino shouldn't be so difficult. She'd been in enough faux embraces with enough handsome male models to know that a touch between a man and a woman could be completely devoid of intimacy, no matter what the camera said. But there was no camera trained on them as she pushed Orsino's collar back off his shoulder, feeling the hot silky smoothness of his skin on her fingertips.

'You'll need to undo the cuff,' he murmured, almost in her ear, and she started, looking down at his wrist.

'Of course.' Poppy fumbled at his cuff and wrenched it undone. With anyone else she'd make a joke of being out of practice undressing men. Not with Orsino.

Swiftly she stripped the shirt off his arm. All she had to do now was see how to get it off his other side. But as her gaze skidded towards his sling she finally took in what the shirt had concealed.

Her throat closed over scratchy sandpaper as she saw the multicoloured bruising that covered every inch of visible skin above the strapping around his ribs. Yellow, green, blue and dull brown, his flesh was a sickening pattern of pain. Poppy blinked, aware of a squeezing in her chest and a dull sensation of nausea in her hollow stomach.

'It looks worse than it is.' Orsino flexed his bare shoulder as if to work out a kink and abruptly Poppy realised she was staring.

'If you say so.' Her voice was brisk as she made herself step around him to undo the knot at his neck that held up his sling.

Inside she felt like crying. Why? She'd seen him in hospital. She knew he was injured. But that wasn't the same as seeing his body so battered.

Her gaze dropped to the wide sweep of his shoulders and back, her belly clenching anew.

Poppy told herself she'd feel the same sympathy for anyone who'd been injured. But this was more profound than sympathy. She tried to reason it wasn't possible, but the truth was too blatant to be ignored. She felt shivery with shock and horror, because it was *Orsino* who was injured.

Despite that snide crack about her sleeping around, despite her pain and anger, when it came to Orsino she still couldn't find a way not to *feel*.

Unbidden the memory of her mother surfaced. She'd tied herself to a man who didn't care about her, and worse, was set on destroying her. She hadn't had the strength to walk away no matter how bad the abuse.

Old creeping fears stirred, whispering a familiar warning that love made you weak.

Poppy shuddered. She was *not* like her mother. She refused to be weak like her, clinging to the wrong man.

Swallowing a knot of emotion, she made her voice cool and businesslike. 'Since they've cut your sleeve away I'll just take the sling off then slide the shirt over your bad arm. Can you hold it still until I tie it up again?'

'Of course.'

Poppy's hands were steady and her movements swift as she stripped the shirt and retied the sling. She showed Orsino the en suite bathroom, put a glass of water on the bedside table and made sure he had everything he needed. She didn't offer to help him out of his trousers.

As she left she congratulated herself. Her moment of weakness had been just that, momentary, no doubt due to shock at being confronted with those bruises.

She could do this: deal with Orsino and put the past behind her. She wasn't susceptible to him. Not any longer.

Poppy squashed the tiny voice that told her life wasn't that simple.

She'd make it simple. It was past time she did.

CHAPTER SIX

ORSINO LET HIMSELF out the tower's big wooden entrance door and stepped into a morning chill with the promise of winter. He drew his coat close.

He'd had enough of being cooped up in luxurious isolation.

His plan had backfired. Instead of having Poppy on tap he was alone most of the day. She left before dawn and returned late.

She couldn't be working all that time. She was avoiding him.

To his chagrin he'd been unable to follow her. He hadn't been nearly as fit as he'd hoped.

Surprisingly, she'd not abandoned him entirely. There'd been short phone calls each day to check he hadn't fallen down the stairs or otherwise damaged himself, and she'd arranged for the catering staff to bring his meals.

All very efficient. Very civilised. Very annoying.

It wasn't some wide-eyed cook he wanted lingering in his presence, or even the curvaceous, sloe-eyed nurse who'd recently removed the sling, leaving the cast on his forearm and fresh bandages on his hand.

He wanted Poppy.

Orsino grimaced. With his strength returning his body made it embarrassingly clear how much he wanted her. With no extreme sport to indulge in, without his usual outlets for rising frustration, Orsino had spent the week in a state of semi-arousal.

Listening to her moving about in the bedroom overhead, smelling her scent on the stairs, hearing the rush of water when she showered and imagining her naked, glistening and beautiful… It was enough to drive a man to drink.

Orsino had no intention of resorting to a bottle to cure what ailed him.

Not when there was another, more pleasing solution.

He peered ahead and noticed activity at the end of the formal rose garden.

Gripping his despised walking stick, he took his time. He could walk without it but he'd learned to his cost that his faulty vision meant he didn't always see obstacles. The last thing he needed was to fall flat on his face in front of Poppy.

It had been a mistake, asking her to help him undress that first day.

What had he thought? That the sight of him half naked would have her desperate for his body?

He grunted and turned onto the riverside path. Serve him right for his inflated ego. She'd taken one look and gone green around the gills. His bruises had repulsed her.

But he had enough experience of women, of Poppy, to know she wasn't impervious. Even after all this time. After how many lovers?

His gut clenched and he faltered midstep. How long had she stayed with Mischa? How many had there been since?

Orsino gritted his teeth. He didn't care. Not any longer. Fortunately his interest now was purely skin-deep.

He slowed, approaching a cluster of people and equipment. Everyone seemed busy, bustling about their various jobs, so he stood unobserved.

At the river's edge a rowboat was pulled up and two people got in. One was a fair-haired man in evening clothes. The other was Poppy. Even from here he recognised her engulfed in that enormous neck-to-ankle coat. Her hair was up but he saw its dark red gleam. Something flashed as she moved in front of a light and he realised she wore a glittering circlet in her hair.

There was a murmur of voices then Poppy shrugged the coat off and Orsino caught his breath.

Her whole dress, what there was of it, danced and sparkled. Knee length, with a deep V neckline at front and back, it caught the light in spangles of silver and blue-green. When she stepped into the boat he saw the skirt was a series of strands that shimmied provocatively around her thighs. Colour glinted at her wrists and throat and high on one arm sat a wide, bright band that looked like a slave bracelet.

She looked coolly elegant, yet gut-wrenchingly sexy, like an untouchable goddess.

But Orsino knew the hot woman who lurked beneath the sophistication. Heat stretched tight bands across his groin and belly.

Over the next hour he watched from a bench seat as the team shot a scene of the pair on the boat, again and again. He couldn't make out the conversation on board, but he heard Poppy's laugh and the murmur of voices—hers and the male model's. He saw the man open a bottle of champagne, heard the crack of the cork, loud as a gunshot, and saw the pair lean close, sipping wine.

And each time a loud voice would interrupt and they'd have to do it all again.

'Look at all that bubbly they're wasting,' groaned a voice nearby.

Orsino turned to see two men, like him, watching the scene on the river.

'It's got to be perfect—you know what the director's like. And they'd better hurry. He wanted the early-morning light.'

'That's no reason to waste good wine.'

'Stop whinging and be thankful you're not stuck in costume for hours, freezing. Look at Poppy Graham out there wearing next to nothing. How many times has she given him his cue and how often has he botched it?'

'Don't waste your sympathy on her, mate. The virgin queen is too uptight to feel the cold.'

'Virgin queen?' Orsino stepped forward and the men turned. The older one stilled, obviously recognising Orsino.

The younger, who'd made the comment, merely nodded and grinned. He was handsome in a plastic sort of way. Orsino wondered if he was a model.

'The unsullied Ms Graham. Colder than an arctic snowstorm she is. God forbid she should let any guy close enough to thaw her.'

'Ah.' Orsino understood now. 'She rebuffed you.'

The other shrugged, ignoring his companion's gesture to be quiet. 'Not just me. She's legendary for it, to the point of being a challenge. I haven't heard of anyone who's struck it lucky with her. There must be ice in her veins, so don't waste your time trying.'

Orsino smiled and wasn't surprised when the man stepped back a pace. He felt like breaking something. Preferably the guy's nose. No doubt it showed.

That brought him up short. Since when did he care what people said of his soon-to-be ex? But the primitive urge to mark his property won out.

'Oh, I won't be wasting my time.' He paused. 'I'm her husband.'

He barely heard the guy's stammered apology as he scurried off. Orsino was too busy trying to work out why fury throbbed through him at the knowledge men wanted to hit on Poppy.

And why she had a reputation for chastity.

Surely after betraying her husband it got easier with each new lover? Unless she was a one-man woman, and she'd found her man in Mischa.

His hands tightened into fists as potent, dark thoughts filled him.

'Ignore him, Mr Chatsfield. He's an idiot. He'd give his

eyeteeth to be out there with your wife, taking the lead in this little extravaganza.'

'I thought it was just a photo shoot.' Orsino forced his mind back from the urge for blood. 'I hadn't realised there was filming, too.'

The other man's eyebrows rose but he was too circumspect to blurt surprise that Poppy hadn't explained.

'There are a series of still shots being taken, but we're making a long ad that will run in cinemas and elsewhere. Baudin has made jewellery for over three hundred years so it's a love story through the centuries. The same couple in different periods. Today it's the roaring twenties.'

Orsino had guessed that much. He nodded to another boat a little downstream.

'It's good to see they take safety so seriously.' The boat contained an oarsman and a diver already kitted out in a wetsuit.

His companion cleared his throat. 'Actually, he's not there to rescue anyone. He's there to retrieve the jewellery if it goes overboard. That armband alone contains several hundred carats in diamonds. It's all vintage Baudin straight from the vault.'

'So the stones are worth more than the models.'

'I wouldn't go that far but—'

'But business is business.' Orsino was glad his business was about people rather than profit.

By the time Poppy came ashore her feet had frozen to blocks of ice in her jewelled shoes. She pressed her lips together so they wouldn't chatter and concentrated on the hot bath she'd promised herself.

The sun was up above the trees now but did little to combat the chill from sitting in silk, beads and little else in the middle of the river. Her hip and thigh ached from lounging artfully on weathered wood and her face was stiff from smiling instead of grimacing with pain. Finally the boat bumped the shore and hands reached for her, holding her steady as she lurched onto dry land.

Soft warmth enveloped her as someone draped a huge coat around her shoulders.

'Thank you.'

Her words were drowned by a burst of laughter. She looked up the slope of the riverbank and blinked. Some of the other models were sprawled on a couple of rugs having what looked like an impromptu breakfast. In the thick of them, like a sultan relaxing with his harem, lounged Orsino, sexier than any male model on set.

He said something and the laughter redoubled. One of the girls rapped him playfully on the shoulder, but Poppy saw her hand linger, stroking. He didn't shift away. Instead his smile widened, that charming smile that could seduce any female. The woman looked dazzled and the rest leaned closer.

Pain jabbed Poppy's ribs, twisting as it went.

She told herself the sight of Orsino charming the pants off her colleagues didn't affect her.

Poppy blinked. *Had* he charmed the pants off one of them? Heat scudded through her at the idea of Orsino with Gretel, or Sasha, or Amy, or…anyone.

Was that why he'd been so undemanding? She'd expected him to make her life hell while he was here. Instead he'd been almost too quiet. She'd assumed his injuries held him back. But maybe his interest was engaged elsewhere. Her breath hissed sharply.

'Poppy?' It was one of the crew. 'Are you okay? You must be half frozen.'

'No, I'm fine. I've warmed up, thanks.' She'd more than warmed. Heat unfurled in her like a great wave, crashing down on her.

Finally she put a name to the emotion that rasped through her like a rusty saw, tearing up her insides, and she despised herself for feeling it. How could she care if Orsino hooked up with another woman under her nose?

As if sensing her regard, Orsino looked up, his smile disappearing. The impact of that look vibrated through her like a plucked string.

Deliberately she turned away.

'Here, take this.' Orsino saw Poppy stiffen at the sound of his voice but she didn't turn.

He didn't enjoy that faint feeling of guilt eddying in his gut. He'd known she was there and had deliberately played up the cosy scene with the models. So why had that one look made him regret his actions? It wasn't that he'd been able to read her expression from that distance. Or that she of all people had any right to judge him.

And yet...

Lips thinning, he walked around to stand before her. 'It's coffee laced with cognac. It will warm you.'

Eyes the colour of dark, crushed violets met his. Makeup accentuated her eyes and turned her lips to a glossy Cupid's bow. She was pure sultry siren yet her expression was blank.

'No drinks till I'm out of this.' She waved a hand down the front of her dress, visible between the folds of her coat. 'Do you have any idea what it's worth?'

As she spoke the woman beside her, retrieving pins from Poppy's hair, removed the glittering headband. Sapphires and diamonds, he guessed. Hair the colour of rich claret cascaded past Poppy's shoulders in a curling tumble.

Something clutched at Orsino's chest. He'd never seen her with her long hair loose. She looked like a medieval princess with attitude.

Then someone nudged him aside to remove her gem-studded bracelets, earrings and matching necklace. Through it all she stood passive, watching him with eyes devoid of interest, as if he just happened to stand where she was looking.

Orsino clenched his teeth, heat stirring in his belly. He

abhorred the fact she'd switched off completely, impervious to him while he still…needed her.

That need was a raw, throbbing ache.

He lifted the coffee to his lips, taking a swig and letting the lacing of alcohol burn its way to his belly.

Before the day was out he'd wipe that condescending blankness from Poppy's face if it was the last thing he did.

Poppy pushed open the door to the tower with a sigh of relief. No work for the rest of the afternoon. Today had been one of the hardest she remembered. So much for throwing herself into her work to avoid Orsino and the way he undermined her certainties.

'Home at last.'

She slammed to a stop. Why wasn't he lolling with his fan club of attentive women? She straightened her shoulders and stepped inside, trying to quell the jittering in her stomach.

Orsino came down the stone staircase, stopping at the bottom.

'You look done in.'

In other words she looked a wreck, as exhausted as she felt. Unlike the other models who'd been preening themselves, vying for his attention. Piercing heat twisted again through her middle.

'Thanks, Orsino,' she snapped. 'Just what I needed to hear.' She shut the door and strode across the foyer.

'What, you'd prefer compliments?' From behind those impenetrable glasses his eyebrows shot up.

'Life's too short to wait for the impossible.'

His mouth cocked up at the corner. 'You know, I could almost come to miss your sassy comebacks.'

Poppy refused to respond to his smile. Work had become a nightmare test of nerves once she became aware of his presence. She carried tension like a weight between her shoulderblades.

'Is there anything in particular you want, Orsino?'

He stood, blocking her way.

'Now there's a question.' His smile grew rakish and the charged air between them sizzled, reigniting the slow burn of resentment she'd felt by the river. To experience that zing of attraction after he'd spent the morning ogling every other woman on-site was the final straw.

'Leave it, Orsino. I'm not in the mood.'

He nodded. 'You've had a difficult day.'

Poppy's eyes rounded. Was he having a dig? It couldn't be genuine sympathy.

'Right. So if you'll excuse me.' She made to go up the stairs but he stood solidly in front of them. A tantalising hint of cedar wood and warm male tickled her nostrils and she quivered, despising herself for the response she couldn't prevent.

'You seem out of sorts.'

Poppy breathed out slowly, trying to banish the scent of him. 'I'm fine.'

'You don't sound it.' He shoved his hands in his pockets, looking as if he had all the time in the world to stand there, annoying her.

She sighed, feeling her control bleeding away. The tension spread from her shoulders now, up the back of her neck. 'I don't know what you want, Orsino, but this isn't the time. Please let me pass.'

'I'm only offering a little sympathy.'

'Sympathy? About my work?' She shook her head. 'That's rich. You always resented it.'

'Perhaps because you used it as an excuse to exclude me.' His voice was silky smooth and all the more irritating for being totally controlled.

'Exclude you?' She gaped. 'You were the one who didn't want to share, going off on your precious expeditions. My work is my career, my livelihood. But you never understood how important that is.' Poppy heaved a choking breath and tried to slow her racing pulse.

How dare he stand there looking smug and superior? He was as much to blame for the disaster their marriage had turned into as she.

'Oh, I understood. Eventually.' He rocked back on his heels. 'When I realised you'd married me for what I could give you: money, position, celebrity. A shortcut on your way to the top.'

Poppy's hands jammed on her hips at the sheer unfairness of that. Fury coiled like a living thing within, writhing to break free. She wouldn't give in to it. Instead she stalked closer, halting when he didn't budge. Without his walking stick or his sling he looked fit as ever. Intimidatingly large and masculine. Undeniably handsome despite the scar from his hairline to his dark glasses. Poppy shivered.

'You look fit enough, Orsino. Maybe it's time for you to move out.'

'Unfortunately my vision will be a handicap for a while yet.' He shrugged casually, setting her teeth on edge. 'Plus it's going to take a while for me to regain my strength.'

'You seem to be managing those stairs just fine. And you don't look in the least weak.'

Orsino crossed his arms over his chest and she saw the bulge of plaster over his forearm beneath his pullover. 'I'm glad you think so.'

He tilted his head to one side as if surveying her better. His hair was just long enough for it to flop over his brow, accentuating the hard perfection of his features.

She hated that she even noticed.

'Why are you so eager for me to leave, Poppy? Don't tell me you're afraid?' His tone was pure provocation.

Poppy had had enough. She moved aside to ascend the stairs. Orsino's good arm shot out, palm flat against the wall, barring her way.

His arm across her breasts felt like a rod of tempered steel but she refused to retreat.

He shifted, crowding her against the wall so she couldn't help but feel defenceless beside his bulk.

Red misted her vision as childhood memories swirled around her.

'Don't throw your weight around with me, Orsino Chatsfield. Just because you're bigger and stronger, you can't bully me.'

She grabbed his arm and tugged but he didn't budge. Hard muscle and raw strength encompassed her and for a frantic instant fear rose. Her breath sawed in her throat as she tried and failed to repress the sense of dark menace bubbling to the surface.

Before she could conquer it, Orsino dropped his arm.

'Poppy?' His wide brow wrinkled.

She swallowed the metallic tang of remembered panic and blinked to clear her vision.

'What is it? What's wrong?'

'Nothing.' She swallowed again. 'Except having you here.'

'I think you're scared.'

His words plunged deep to the heart of her, to the place she'd kept hidden for years. The place no one but her mother had known about.

Her chin jutted as she looked up at him. Why did he have to goad and prod and interfere?

Why did he have to come back into her life, disrupting her hard-won peace after all this time?

Her nerves were shattered after a week with him under the same roof, evoking memories of a time when she'd na-ively thought herself the luckiest woman in the world.

Worse, she'd found herself *jealous* today, seeing him with other women. Jealous of the man who'd almost destroyed her! She couldn't stand him and yet he made her feel things she shouldn't. Her skin felt too tight, as if there was something inside, bursting to get out.

'Scared? Of you?' Poppy all but spat the words. She drilled her index finger into his chest, pushing that wall of solid muscle. 'Think again, Orsino. There's nothing you can do to me now.'

Nothing worse than abandoning her when she'd needed him most.

'If you're not scared of me then of what?' His voice deepened and she felt it like a caress on her skin, making her quiver. He reached for his glasses and suddenly she was looking into ebony eyes that seemed to see right into her. The glasses clattered to the floor. 'Of this?'

His head dipped, slowly, as if he expected her to pull back. But her legs seemed to have planted themselves and her heartbeat, instead of racing with anger, slowed to a sluggish, heavy throb of anticipation.

Poppy told herself to move, now, but nothing happened. Until Orsino's mouth met hers and that expectant quiver became a shudder of pleasure.

Hunger slammed into her with a force that knocked all memory of the past from her mind. His lips were warm, firm and insistent, parting her mouth before she realised she should have stopped him. His tongue danced against hers, inviting her to join him, tempting her to pleasure. The taste of him was like all her 'if onlys' rolled into one.

Her hands inched up his broad chest to his shoulders, fingers sinking into fine cashmere and male heat. His hand anchored her head, demanding more as he bowed her back towards the wall.

Orsino's mouth on hers was devastatingly familiar yet the urgency was new, heady and acute. It spiralled inside her from a place that had been dormant so long she'd thought it dead.

Need exploded with an intensity that couldn't be denied.

It swamped her, driving her against Orsino, begging him for more with her hands and mouth and her body.

He groaned deep in his throat, the sound kindling a spark that caught and flared in her blood. Orsino shifted his head for better access as she moved, too. Urgency made them clumsy, teeth catching flesh in their hunger for more.

Hands plucked at soft cashmere. Thighs shifted, slipping apart. Soft breast to hard torso, they strained together, driven by a storm that ripped apart caution and self-preservation.

Orsino's hand was at her breast, his thumb swiping her beaded nipple, sending ripples of ecstasy through her body in tiny electric jolts.

Poppy's hands slid down, around his back, clutching the taut bunching of his buttocks through soft denim. Fingers splayed, she pressed closer, right into that deliciously heavy ridge of arousal. Her chest thumped hard and seemed to melt at the rightness of it.

'Yes,' he hissed in her mouth. And 'Yes' again as he ground his pelvis in a tight circle against her. Scorching heat engulfed her as she gasped.

It had been so long.

She'd forgotten, had thought her memories had enhanced the excruciating delight of Orsino's body melding with hers.

A tiny voice in the back of her head squawked about weakness and danger. But this wasn't weakness. She felt suddenly, gloriously powerful. Strength and pleasure coursed in her veins, pure and unadulterated. Her grasp on his backside tightened, pulling him close.

'Help me.' Orsino's voice was a ragged gasp barely audible over the thrum of her pulse. His hand fumbled at her waist, fingers grazing her skin as he wrestled with the catch on her trousers. Ripples of sensation rayed out across her abdomen and up to her breasts.

'Help me!' His voice was hoarse with frustration, echoing her own rising desperation.

Her fingers found his belt, sliding it free, ripping at the button on his jeans.

His ragged breathing was hot in Poppy's ears as her trousers slid to the floor. A flurry of urgent movement and she was naked from the waist down, clothes discarded. In their place was Orsino, his hand doing things that made her eyes flutter shut and her breath clog.

'Yes!' Her voice was high and breathless as she peeled away denim and took him in her hand. So hot, so silky and strong.

Orsino yanked her thigh high over his hip and she felt the wall hard at her back. Hands to his shoulders she rose, her eyes snapping open to meet the blaze of his as he surged beneath her, filling her with heat and power till he reached the core of her.

For a suspended millisecond she froze, shocked at the acute pleasure.

Then Orsino roared something in Italian. Their bodies arched frantically and when he thrust again she felt his urgent pulse of completion. Hot seed exploded within and still he powered into her, forcing her to the brink of ecstasy till the world caught fire and she shattered into a thousand glittering shards.

CHAPTER SEVEN

POPPY'S HEAD FLOPPED against Orsino's shoulder, her heart thundering, pleasure still coursing through her in tiny waves that rippled right to the tips of her fingers and toes.

His broad hand held her bare leg. His thighs wedged solid beneath her, supporting her, and his laboured gasps were hot in her hair.

He shifted a fraction and one last spasm racked her. She bit her lip against the cry of delight that rose to her lips. But he knew. His hand tightened possessively.

She squeezed her eyes shut. What nonsense! As if Orsino cared.

'Poppy?' His voice was a low burr of sound that abraded her like a rough caress. It made her skin tingle in places that had just come alive for the first time in five years.

Five years. She hadn't been with a man before or since Orsino and now, like a piece of ripe fruit, she fell into his hands. How could she have done it?

Horror and shame washed through her.

How self-destructive could she be, giving herself to a man who despised her? The man who'd almost destroyed her?

Hands shoving at his chest she wriggled till he stepped back and she half slid down to the floor, ignoring the sharp pang of loss and protest from her wayward body. Her knees were so weak she'd have collapsed if it wasn't for Orsino, holding her steady.

Heat scorched her cheeks as she looked down. One foot bare, the other still shod, and with her trousers tangled around that ankle.

'I can't believe I did that.'

'Believe it, Poppy.' Something in his voice jerked her head up. Eyes she knew to be dark brown glittered almost black. She expected smug satisfaction, even triumph in his expression, but found something else. Something she couldn't name.

A pulse of connection passed between them, like in the old days when she'd felt a oneness with him that she'd believed utterly precious.

Old guilt swirled in a clogging tide. No matter how much Orsino was to blame for the destruction of their marriage, it was she who'd taken that first irrevocable step, in her grief and loneliness turning to Mischa for comfort. Even if she *had* pulled back before she broke her wedding vows.

'Poppy?' Orsino's voice broke her thoughts. 'It's not the end of the world.'

She hiccupped on welling laughter. Orsino comforting her? Impossible.

'Of course it's not.' She forced herself to meet his eyes again. 'But it's still unbelievable.' She scrabbled at her feet, wriggling her bare foot into her clothes and dragging them up rather than stand half naked before him.

By the time she'd finished his jeans were zipped up, too.

Another wash of heat flamed at the realisation he hadn't even had to shuck his jeans off to take her. And she'd let him. More than let him, she'd egged him on, climbing his tall frame in her hunger for him. Her internal muscles clenched at the memory and she shivered.

Poppy tilted her chin, projecting haughty confidence to cover the way she trembled.

'Pleasant as it's been, Orsino, I need to—'

'Running, Poppy?' He arched one eyebrow, lifting the still-raw-looking scar that curled around his eye.

'We're done here.' How she got the words out she didn't know. But she had to get away before what was left of her composure crumbled entirely.

'If I didn't know better I'd call that statement naive.'

Her eyes widened. Orsino calling her naive? Last she'd heard she was the scarlet woman incarnate.

'Look, Orsino. You've had your—' she waved an arm as she searched for words '—gratification.' How he must be silently crowing at the fact she'd succumbed to him so easily. 'But it's over and it won't happen again. Now I'd like to go and have a shower.'

'Of course it's going to happen again.' Slowly he shook his head, the look in his eyes doing silly things to her insides. 'But next time had better be somewhere more comfortable. I told you I hadn't got my strength back.' He rolled his shoulder and shifted his arm, reminding her of the plaster cast he still wore.

Poppy stared, torn between asking if he'd injured himself and the memory of his strength as he'd held her high, pounding into her till ecstasy claimed them both.

The touch of his fingertips on her cheek stopped her as she made to brush past him. So gentle, yet that caress made her breath hitch and that squirming, hungry ache begin again in her stomach.

'You can't run from this, Poppy. It's not going away.' His fingers feathered down to stroke her swollen lips. 'If you prefer, I could provoke you into another fight so you have an excuse to release all that tension and let yourself go. But it would be so much more fun if you accepted it.'

'Fun?' Her voice rose to a screech. 'I'm not interested in having *fun* with you, Orsino.' She'd just betrayed herself.

His eyes narrowed. 'You're not trying to say that hot, hungry sex we just shared was about love, are you?' He said *love* as if it was a sour taste on his tongue.

'Of course not. This was just…' She gestured vaguely.

'Pure animal desire.' His voice dropped to a rough caress. 'White-hot sex that blows the back off your head and leaves you a quivering wreck.'

He didn't look a quivering wreck. He looked raffishly handsome and sure of himself.

'The sort of sex that—'

'Enough, enough!' She raised her hand. 'The way you're going on about it anyone would think you hadn't been with a woman in years.'

His face stiffened into rigid lines and he drew himself up, looming above her.

'I'm facing facts, Poppy.' He took her wrist, fingers against the frantic throb of her pulse. 'This isn't going away. Don't you understand?'

'It has to.' Did she sound as desperate as she felt?

She wrenched her hand away and crossed her arms, counteracting the chill that gripped her. 'We have nothing in common except a train wreck of a relationship.' She wouldn't go there again.

'You still don't see. I'm not talking about a *relationship*.' Again that bitter emphasis. 'This is lust, pure and simple.'

'But we don't *like* each other.' She groped for the words that would end this farce. 'You detest me.' She swallowed hard, telling herself it no longer mattered.

Orsino tilted his head and that lock of hair tumbled forward. Poppy's fingers twitched. She wanted to brush it back, feel its softness.

'I'll cut you a deal, Poppy. I won't mention the past if you don't. It has no bearing on this.' His gesture encompassed the pair of them and the wall where he'd just given her the most exciting climax of her life. 'The past is behind us. *But* the physical attraction isn't. Why not enjoy it? Why not let it run its course so when we part this time it will be completely over? Then there won't be any lingering shreds of…connection.'

She stared, not believing what she heard.

'You can't be serious!'

'Never more so.' He raised his brows, managing to look impossibly superior. 'That's the difference between men and women. Men are pragmatic. We can distinguish lust from affection. What you and I share is steaming-hot physical desire.'

As he spoke a pulse started up high between her legs.

'You feel it, don't you?' His eyes gleamed, the lids lowering as he gave her a look that turned her knees to jelly.

She shook her head. 'Once was more than enough.'

'Liar,' he taunted. 'That barely touched the surface and you know it. All it did was bring this out into the open. Now it will be even harder to ignore.' He paused as if waiting for her to reply but her tongue was stuck to the roof of her mouth.

'At least think about it.'

He waited till she finally, reluctantly, nodded—anything to end this conversation. Then to her relief he moved back, giving her access to the staircase.

Her foot was on the first step when he spoke again.

'One last thing.' He paused. 'I didn't use protection. Do I have anything to worry about?'

It took far too long for Poppy to fathom his meaning. When she did, it was with a sick churning in her stomach.

He hadn't used protection.

She hadn't even thought about it. How could she have been so caught up in desire that she hadn't noticed? It was as if an irresponsible stranger had taken over her body.

It was on the tip of Poppy's tongue to announce she hadn't been with anyone since him but she thought better of it. He wouldn't believe it, or if by some miracle she could convince him, he'd see it as a sign she carried a torch for him.

'No.' Her voice was low. 'You've got nothing to worry about on that score. But what about me? Are you safe?' She remembered his multitude of partners in all those press reports and her insides tightened.

'Don't worry. I'm clean as a whistle.' Yet the tension around his mouth told her there was something on his mind.

She waited but he said nothing about the risk of pregnancy.

Of course. He assumed she'd have that covered. No doubt he imagined her hopping from bed to bed. Frantically she calculated dates in her head, reassuring herself the chances of pregnancy were slim.

That was another reason to veto his proposition. Getting pregnant to her ex would be a mistake even more momentous than her error in marrying him.

Slowly she hauled herself up the stairs, conscious of Orsino's eyes on her. Shame filled Poppy at the needy ache between her legs, sign of the weakness he'd reawakened within her.

Yet even in the privacy of her room she couldn't get his outrageous suggestion out of her head. It had a terrible, seductive logic, which just showed how off balance she was.

She'd once made a catastrophic mistake, believing love could conquer all, despite what she knew about love turning women into victims. She'd loved Orsino with a passion that overrode sense, marrying him in a whirlwind of excitement. She'd ignored the voice of warning, telling herself their love would make it right.

But it hadn't been *their* love, had it? It had been hers alone. She'd fallen head over heels for him. But Orsino? He'd always held part of himself back, maintaining a depth of reserve masked by charm and potent sexuality.

History had repeated itself. First her parents then her and Orsino.

Loving and losing had almost destroyed her. She couldn't countenance the idea of giving herself in love again.

So if not love, what about lust? Was there sense in Orsino's words? She couldn't shake the insidious idea he might be right.

Maybe she could practise what he preached, take lovers

to assuage this hunger he'd reawakened. In five years she hadn't managed to eradicate him. Could a no-holds-barred sexual relationship do what abstinence hadn't and free her once and for all?

Poppy showered so long the flesh on her fingers started to pucker, but no answer presented itself. Common sense and the voice of temptation raced round her head, like mice on a never-ending wheel.

Slicking back the weight of wet hair from her face she turned off the water then leaned, palms braced, against the tiled shower wall. She'd thought to wash off Orsino's touch and scent, but the warm spray of water had only energised her still-aroused body, making her regret the speed of what had happened downstairs. She hadn't felt his touch on her bare skin and, tucked away in the privacy of her bathroom, she admitted the truth—that she wanted that, wanted Orsino, more than anything.

Poppy squeezed her eyes shut, berating herself. This wouldn't do.

Reaching out for the shower door she instead encountered hot flesh. Bare hot flesh with a delicious smattering of crisp hair.

Her eyes sprang open.

'Orsino!'

One look at her and Orsino knew he'd been right to come. Without time to don her touch-me-not hauteur, Poppy's expression betrayed her. The dreamy yearning in her eyes, the ripe invitation of her parted lips, the way she swayed towards him instead of recoiling.

Oh, yes, she wanted him as he did her. That went some way towards silencing his concerns about the immensity of his hunger for her.

The feel of her damp palm splaying over his chest made his heart erupt in a tattoo of need.

'Who else?' His voice was unsteady as his gaze dropped

to her delicious body, glowing softly from the heat of the shower. High, pert breasts that made his palms ache to hold them. Dark raspberry nipples. A long, lithe sweep of torso down to a waist that he knew fitted his hands perfectly. The purely feminine curve of hips cradling that dark russet triangle of soft hair. He swallowed convulsively, remembering the taste of her on his tongue. Slender, strong legs and narrow, sexy feet.

'Here.' He took her by the elbow, guiding her out of the shower cubicle. 'Let me.' He lifted the enormous bath towel he held and draped it around her shoulders, pulling her closer.

'You shouldn't be here. I didn't invite you.' He heard her reaching for indignation but she couldn't quite achieve it.

And they both knew why.

'Where else would I be?' Slowly he rubbed her shoulders through the plush towelling. 'I want you. And you want me.' He paused, waiting. 'Don't you, Poppy?'

Her breath hitched and her dazed eyes grew heavy-lidded as his hands found her breasts through the thick towel.

She opened her mouth but no sound emerged. He would have grinned in triumph at finally silencing her sassy tongue, but he felt like she looked, poleaxed.

'It's not *you*.' She grabbed his hands and dragged them away. 'As you explained so clearly, it's just sex.'

He watched her cheeks flush and something tightened inside. That blush of hers had fascinated him from the first. He'd assumed a woman who displayed her body in swimsuits and skimpy dresses would have lost the ability to blush. Not Poppy.

The first time he'd stripped her naked the rosy heat in her cheeks had been adorable, and he'd actually wondered if he might be her first lover. Until she'd responded with such unabashed enthusiasm he'd realised how impossible that was.

She cleared her throat. 'It's been a while for me, that's all. That's why I...'

'So it isn't me you want? Anyone would do? Is that what you're saying?' Orsino pulled back, watching a tiny frown wrinkle her forehead. 'There was a guy this morning, one of the models, who'd love to be here, helping you scratch this particular itch. Maybe you should call him instead.'

Where the poisonous words came from Orsino didn't know. Maybe a last-ditch effort to slice through the final bond linking them.

Yet as he spoke a dagger of heat plunged deep at the thought of Poppy with another man. Even now. Even after all this time. Hell!

He forced himself to withdraw back towards the bedroom door.

As he did her gaze drifted down his body and her eyes widened as she saw him naked and, despite his fury, fully aroused. His muscles clenched with the effort it took not to reach out and drag her to him.

He needed her but he refused to beg.

Poppy stared at his erection as if she'd never seen one before and he felt himself pulse, hard and eager.

Half an hour ago he'd almost embarrassed himself. He would have climaxed in her hand in another few seconds. He'd only just managed to wait till he was inside her before shattering like a kid with his first woman. He'd told himself abstinence was the cause, next time he'd be in control, yet he found himself wondering if he might come just from watching her sultry eyes devour him.

She swallowed convulsively and heat poured through him. He remembered that mouth like hot velvet on his aroused body, reducing him to gasping surrender. He wanted that again. He wanted—

Her eyes snared his and a wave of something crashed over him. Not just desire, but something deeper. Something he thought he'd banished.

'Is that what you want?' he snarled. 'Someone else to relieve your...tension?' When she said nothing he forced himself on, refusing to feel the pain of her rejection. 'Maybe while you're at it you could see if one of the women from this morning would like to do something about *this*—' he gestured to his erection '—since you're not interested.'

Poppy jerked her head away. Orsino's eyes narrowed. He couldn't trust his damaged vision but he'd swear he caught the glitter of tears on her lashes.

'Poppy?' His voice was husky as he spoke over what felt like broken glass lining his throat.

She turned back and he realised she'd been biting her bottom lip. It was dark and swollen and he wanted to soothe it with his thumb.

'All right. You win, Orsino. I admit it.' Her voice was low. 'It's you I want, not just any man.' She crossed the floor till they stood toe to toe and her hand found his chest again, making his heart judder. 'Satisfied?'

Her chin tilted high as it always had when she was scared. Heat doused him as he realised it.

Poppy was scared?

That knowledge sliced through his anger, leaving him strangely hollow.

Orsino covered her hand with his, feeling it quiver like a wounded bird in his grasp.

'Not yet.' His voice had turned to gravel. 'Because I need you so badly I can't think straight. Not just any woman but *you*, Poppy. Just you.'

A last remnant of pride howled that he gave too much away, letting her know the power she wielded. But for once the urge for honesty overrode it.

'Don't cry, Poppy. It's not just you feeling this. It's me, too.'

'Really?' She blinked up at him and her eyes shone over-bright, making him feel about ten inches tall for the way he'd behaved.

For so long he'd wanted her to suffer for what she'd done. Yet, seeing her distress, he realised he couldn't face it.

'It's not the way I want it to be, either,' he admitted. 'But it's the way it is. For now.' He dragged in a deep breath. 'I need you, Poppy. Just you.'

'And I need you, Orsino.' He barely heard the words but he felt the soft puff of her breath on his bare flesh as she spoke. 'Only you.'

Orsino made himself ignore the way that sounded almost like a vow. This was simple physical attraction. And the sooner they sated it, the better.

He drew her into the bedroom and lay her down with exquisite care on the bedspread. He feared one wrong move and he'd lose what little control he had left.

'I love your hair,' he admitted as he splayed the wet tendrils wide, like a fan of rich garnet.

'I love yours.' Her hand went to his forehead, brushing it back where it threatened to flop over his forehead.

Her touch was light, barely there, yet he felt it with a force that made something sing within him. That's what Poppy did to him, what she'd always done to him.

'Say it again.'

'I want you, Orsino.' Her hand traced a line of fire across his new scar. She traced it down to his eye then slid her hand up and into his hair and his heart thudded. 'I need you.'

'Good.' He tried to smile but the tension in him was too great. He clasped the back of her hand and turned his face to press a kiss to her palm. 'So in this we're equals.'

After a moment she nodded and he moved away.

At her gasp of distress he did manage a smile after all. 'I'm just getting this.' He held up the box of condoms he'd put on her bedside table while she showered.

There was that blush again across her breasts and throat.

Possessiveness filled him. She'd admitted her hunger was for him alone, but he knew an overwhelming urgency to banish Poppy's previous lovers from her mind.

His body wasn't as strong as he liked. Plaster encased one forearm and one hand still didn't work properly, but that didn't prevent him lavishing the attention on her that she deserved.

Orsino planted tiny kisses up her rib cage, feeling her shiver and shift beneath him, then nuzzled the fragrant, soft skin of her throat where a pulse beat frantically. The scent of berries and aroused woman grew headier as he lavished kisses down her other side, pausing low on her hip where a tiny heart-shaped scar had always fascinated him.

With lips and tongue and hands he explored her supple legs, the groove at the back of her knees, where she was so sensitive he had to hold her steady, using his weight to anchor her.

He loved her writhing beneath him, a prelude to what was to come.

Smiling, he inched his way up her thighs, fingers trailing a butterfly-light tracery across tender ivory flesh.

She gasped when he reached the junction of her thighs, her legs parting beneath him.

'So eager,' he crooned, blown away as he always had been by Poppy's unabashed sexuality. She gave herself up to him completely. He hadn't let himself remember that in five years. Now the reality of her in the flesh was almost too much. He longed to slide up her body and thrust hard and fast till they dissolved in ecstasy.

But he was determined to imprint himself on her. He'd make sure she knew at the deepest level it was him giving her what she needed.

Poppy tasted sweet and salty, a tang of pure feminine delight on his tongue and lips. He nuzzled closer, enjoying her hoarse gasps and the way she held his head in tight fingers that betrayed everything she felt.

One last, long, luxurious lick and she bucked hard beneath him, right off the bed, only his body weight holding her steady.

He felt shudders race through her, jerking her limbs, and saw the bright flare of ecstasy under her skin. But it was the way she cried his name, like a benediction and a plea together, that unlocked something he couldn't name.

Finally, when she lay still beneath him, he rose to lie beside her on the bed. Her eyes fluttered open and the drowsy contentment he read there warmed him in places he'd forgotten existed.

'Now, Orsino.' Her lips curved in a tiny, siren's smile.

'But I've only just started.' His hand slid to that damp triangle of dark curls as his head bent to her breast and he finally allowed himself the freedom to suckle her breast.

It was a long time later when Orsino finally rose on his elbows above her.

His body throbbed with the tension of denying his own gratification so long, and with the effort required of his still-recuperating body, but it was worth it.

Poppy was his, branded by touch and taste and climax after climax till there could be no doubt in her mind or her heart that she was his.

Orsino stilled, frowning. This wasn't about hearts.

She lay limp beneath him, her body glowing and perfect as he held her close and slowly, excruciatingly slowly, slid home.

Her eyelids rose, her expression the sweetest he'd ever seen. Warm arms wrapped around his back, soft legs tightened at his waist. And suddenly, before Orsino had a chance to feel triumph, his body surged high and hard, his breath ragged as he reached breaking point. With a great roar of pleasure his head arched back and his climax broke upon him, wave after wave of crashing ecstasy.

When finally he came to his senses he was a dead weight crushing her to the bed, his head cradled against her damp, scented neck, his heart thundering against her, her name echoing in the still air.

Reluctantly he dragged himself up on his elbows, despite her clinging hold. His ribs ached but he didn't care. He lowered his head, not ready to meet her eyes. One thing was certain. If their loving had branded her as his, the process worked two ways. He felt bound to Poppy as he hadn't for five years.

How did that fit with his plan to bed her and walk away?

CHAPTER EIGHT

'No, I CAN'T, BETTINA. That's the trouble.'

Poppy paused just inside the tower door and let it swing shut behind her. The simmering frustration in Orsino's voice caught her attention.

Who was Bettina? What had she done to make him so edgy?

Jealousy stabbed Poppy between the ribs and she knew a terrible fear at the realisation.

For four nights she'd shared Orsino's bed. Nights of frantic passion, untold bliss and early mornings of languorous loving that left her glowing.

She should be horrified and ashamed that she'd capitulated, giving herself to Orsino again. But somehow she'd managed to block out the voice of doom that sniped in her ear. She got through each day hour by hour, not letting herself think beyond the moment.

From the open door to the sitting room she heard Orsino's tread, heavy across the ancient floor.

'I've tried that but—' A loud clatter made her jump. Orsino swore. 'No, no, I'm fine, Bettina. Sorry. It's these damned eyes. I can see, almost, but every so often I misjudge distances and walk into things.'

There was a pause and the sound of scraping.

'No, that wasn't the laptop. I almost wish it was—it's driving me crazy.' Another pause. 'I know, I know, patience.' He spoke on a long sigh that dragged across her skin.

Poppy moved till she saw Orsino, silhouetted against the lowering grey sky through the window. His shoulders were hunched as he thrust one hand through his hair.

A tingle of heat swarmed up her backbone and her stomach muscles clenched, just from the pleasure of watching him.

That had to be bad. When just looking at him made her body react.

Her lips firmed. There was nothing wrong with enjoying physical attraction, the new Poppy told herself, so long as it was just that. Nothing...complicated by emotions.

They'd finished shooting early when the threatening skies had finally opened in a downpour and she'd hurried back here, brushing off an invitation to join the others.

It struck her as she drank in the sight of Orsino's big, bold frame that she'd never questioned how he occupied his time while she worked. They'd each been careful not to extend their conversation beyond what happened in the bedroom. But knowing Orsino and his appetite for action, being cooped here without something to do was way out of character.

Now she felt overwhelming curiosity. About what was on that laptop. And about Bettina.

She stepped closer and his head snapped round. Poppy rocked back on her heels as their gazes locked and desire punched hard and low.

Just like that!

Wanton images filled her head. She and Orsino tangled together on the wide couch below the mullioned window. Orsino naked on the rug before the crackling fire, beckoning her close. The dark fire in his eyes as he drove her to climax then held her as the world faded into a blur.

'Don't worry, Bettina. I'll try again later. Bye.' He didn't sound in the least loverlike.

Poppy told herself his relationships didn't matter to her.

But she lied. Was Bettina his lover? Distress squirmed in her belly. She schooled her face to hide it.

'You're back early.'

She shrugged, nodding to the rain pelting against the glass. 'We filmed outdoors but the weather beat us. We'll work inside tomorrow.'

He slipped his phone away and shoved his hands into his pockets. He didn't reach for her and she wondered if she'd intruded on something. His wary stance put her senses on alert.

Deliberately she wandered closer, looking casually towards the enormous fireplace, noting the laptop open on an ottoman and a bundle of papers on the arm of a wing chair.

She kept her expression neutral as she met his eyes. No dark glasses today.

With a flick of deft fingers she undid her coat and shrugged it off, trailing it over the back of a tapestry-upholstered chair. Something flickered across his face and was gone.

'You don't seem pleased to see me, Orsino. Am I interrupting something?' She was close enough now to see he wasn't as unaffected as he pretended. His gaze was riveted on her lips, still a glossy rich crimson from today's shoot. His big hands clenched at his sides and his chest rose mightily as if he struggled to inhale enough oxygen.

Good. She'd hate to be the only one feeling needy.

'Orsino?' Poppy paused, letting her mouth form a musing pout and feeling a pulse of satisfaction at his distracted stare. She moved closer, wondering if it would be too obvious if she slicked her tongue over her mouth.

Why not? Tentatively she swiped the tip of her tongue over her lower lip. His jaw tightened and cords of tension appeared in his neck.

It was deliciously empowering, knowing Orsino was as vulnerable to her as she was to him.

She told herself that was all she wanted: a purely physical relationship. So where her next words came from she didn't know.

'I couldn't help overhearing. Is there some problem with your computer?'

Orsino's face was blank, only his eyes were alive, fixed on her mouth with an intensity that sent arousal glissading through her.

'Orsino? Have I got lipstick on my teeth?'

'No.' His voice was a scraping bass note that made her skin prickle and her nipples tighten. 'You have the sexiest mouth I've ever seen. I can't get enough of it.'

Poppy blinked, stunned at his admission. Generous lover though he was, he rarely hinted at the depth of his passion. He let his body do that.

'In that case—' she drew an unsteady breath '—I'll make sure you get all you want.' Poppy stepped in, skimmed a light kiss across his lips then moved away, her eyes drifting deliberately down his tense body. It trembled beneath her gaze and she smiled.

Oh, yes, she *did* enjoy the pure no-holds-barred physicality of this new relationship.

'Witch.' His voice was husky. The fine hairs along her neck and arms rose in response.

She arched her eyebrows. 'You enjoy it. You know you do.'

His mouth tugged up at one side, a long dimple cleaving his cheek. It was Poppy's turn to stare, transfixed by the masculine potency of that smile.

She cleared her throat. 'Your laptop. Is it damaged? I heard something fall.'

Orsino stepped back, arms folding over his chest.

'No. I walked into a side table. My vision's still not right.'

'Give it time,' she found herself urging. 'You always were impatient.'

His eyes narrowed and she wondered if he'd accuse her of overstepping some imaginary line. Instead he nodded, one hand plunging through his hair again, leaving it rumpled and effortlessly sexy.

'So everyone says.'

'Bettina, too?'

'You heard?' For a moment she wondered if his brows would descend in a scowl because she'd eavesdropped. Instead he shrugged. 'The woman has the patience of Job. She has to have, working with me. She can't see why I'm not the same.'

'She's your secretary?' Bubbles of something—relief?—fizzed in Poppy's bloodstream. Not another woman then.

He nodded. 'Though for how much longer if I can't pull my act together, I don't know.'

'It can't be that bad, surely.' Organising one of Orsino's mountaineering trips would take effort but surely it wasn't that complicated.

His mouth flattened as his hand slid down to scrub the back of his neck. 'It is when I can't read vital documents and decisions need to be made.'

'Can I help?'

The words were out before she realised it. They took him by surprise too, given the look on his face.

'Help?' He made it sound like a foreign word.

'With the laptop. If you're having trouble opening the document…'

He shook his head. 'Oh, I can open it. For an inveterate adventure seeker I'm surprisingly techno-savvy.' His lips quirked up in a dry half smile. 'The trouble is my vision.' His voice faded on the last word as if it was something he didn't want to admit. Despite herself, Poppy felt something clutch inside her at that unexpected evidence of his vulnerability.

He'd always hated admitting weakness. The fact that he shared this now seemed ridiculously important. She told herself she was imagining things and forced herself to focus.

'Would you like me to read it to you?'

His hand dropped to his side and his brows arrowed in a frown.

'That would be…' Abruptly he shook his head. 'Thank you. But no. It's a big document, a spreadsheet, not an email.'

Curiouser and curiouser. What sort of spreadsheets would Orsino need?

Then the reason for his hesitation hit her. It probably detailed his impressive income and investment portfolio.

Who would want to share that with his soon-to-be-ex-wife just prior to their divorce?

Poppy waved her hand. 'It was just a thought. Don't worry about it.'

He stepped forward and the scent of heady spice and cedar infiltrated her brain. How she'd miss that when they went their separate ways.

'You'd really do that? It's tedious stuff.'

She spread her hands. 'I've finished early. My time is my own.'

Yet she was offering to spend it with Orsino. Not indulging in hot, frantic sex, but to read him a spreadsheet. What had got into her? What had happened to keeping her distance?

'It can't be worse than wearing a corset for hours, waiting for my leading man to get his lines right.'

'That bad, eh?' A glimmer of amusement lit Orsino's dark eyes and it struck her how attractive his smile was. Not just sexy but…appealing.

'You have no idea.' She took a deep breath and stretched, revelling in the freedom of minimal underwear after the restrictions of the outfit she'd worn today.

Orsino's gaze dropped to snag on her breasts and instantly her nipples beaded, pushing against the thin fabric of her T-shirt. Excitement ignited deep inside and spread, making her quiver.

Poppy dropped her arms and turned to the fireplace. The intensity of that reaction was too unsettling.

'You want me to read this document?'

'That would be helpful, thanks.' Unlike hers Orsino's voice was cool and even. Had she imagined that hungry stare?

'Sure.' Eager for distraction, she moved away and dropped cross-legged before the padded ottoman where his computer sat. He took the big wing chair just behind her. If she leaned back his legs would support her.

Poppy squashed a stray thought about how cosy this was, the sound of the rain battering the windows and a fire throwing warmth across the Oriental rug. Just her and Orsino...

With a sharp intake of breath she blinked and reached for the computer. Daydreaming about relaxed evenings by the fire with her husband wasn't healthy. Once she'd mistaken his passion for love. She needed to keep her wits about her and remember the rules.

Ignore the past, since it hurts too much.
Ignore the future, since we have none.
Live in the now.
Keep it simple.

Her heart lurched as for a moment forbidden memories invaded—hurtful memories. Then she slammed a lid on them. Better to pretend those were two different people than tear herself apart trying to explain how she could want Orsino and he her after what had gone before.

'What document did you want me to read?'

Orsino leaned forward and took the laptop from her hands, clicking through files.

Trying not to react to his beckoning heat, she stared at the screen. All the documents were enlarged for easy reading.

'You can't read that?' Poppy looked at the large font and her heart sank. She'd thought his vision was improving. He seemed so capable now, able to move about with ease.

Though it struck her that she rarely saw him anywhere but in bed or the bathroom.

A cool little ripple cascaded down her spine.

'I can read those.' After a little fumbling he opened a document and passed the laptop to her. 'But following the lines and footnotes on this spreadsheet is beyond me.' He paused and she felt his breath warm on the back of her neck where she'd piled her hair up. 'My sight is still distorted and it makes this stuff too difficult.'

'I'm not surprised.' Vast rows and columns of figures filled the page. 'You really need to do this now?' Surely it was better for him to rest and recuperate.

'If you've changed your mind—'

'No. Of course not. Which worksheet do you want?'

'Might as well start at the first. Can you start at the top and work your way down?'

It didn't take long to realise the report had nothing to do with blue-chip investments or property. Nor was it about climbing or rally car racing or any of the extreme sports for which Orsino was feted.

'Can you go back a line?' She heard the scratching of pen on paper. He could see enough to write then. The tightness in her chest unravelled a little.

She recited dates and figures. 'What is this, Orsino?'

There was silence for a few moments apart from the scratch of his pen and the soft thunk of embers in the fire.

'Expenses. Medical treatment. Food. Maintenance.'

'I gathered that.' She peered at the figures again. 'But for whom?'

'For an establishment I deal with. Now, if you'd—'

'What sort of establishment?'

Orsino's reluctance to talk intrigued her. What was he hiding? And even more intriguing, what had happened to the man who barely stood still long enough even for a wedding photo? Who now found the patience to sit churning through reams of figures?

'Orsino?'

He shifted behind her as if the chair was no longer comfortable.

'It's a rehabilitation centre.'

'For...?' This was like drawing a tooth.

'For people who've been injured by landmines.'

Poppy put the laptop down and swung around.

He ignored her while he scrawled another note in large capitals.

'And?'

Finally the pen stopped and he looked up, his face unreadable.

'Why are you going through these reports?'

He shrugged those mouth-wateringly broad shoulders but this time Poppy kept her eyes on his face, sensing this was significant.

'You know my expeditions raise money for charity.'

'I do.' Her heart had been in her mouth more than once as she'd watched him succeed at some daredevil stunt, filmed from a distance and broadcast on television. 'But what's that got to do with this—' she waved her hand '—administration?'

She didn't need to spell it out. He wasn't a desk jockey. He was action man, always on the move, always with new conquests to make.

'Careful administration is what keeps these enterprises ticking over. Without oversight they could face disaster. This way we know the money is going where it's needed.'

'We?'

He sat back and rubbed his eyes. Poppy's chest tightened in sympathy. Perhaps she should back off, but she sensed if she didn't pursue this now she'd never learn more. Those impenetrable steel walls would slam down, shutting her out.

She didn't stop to question why she needed to pry his secret loose.

'The board that manages them.'

'You're on a management board?'

'Several of them.' His lips twisted in a wry grimace. 'Unbelievable, huh?'

Poppy stared at the man she'd once thought she knew. Strong, determined, energetic, focused to the point of single-mindedness, a man who made things happen instead of sitting on the sidelines.

'Not at all. I can see that you'd be a valuable addition.'

His eyes widened and his dark brows shot up.

'How did you get involved?'

Orsino sat back, his gaze sliding towards the gathering darkness outside. Obviously this wasn't something he often spoke about. The fact that he shared with *her* created a warm jiggle in the pit of her stomach.

'I did a favour for a friend. He wanted a companion to paddle across the Timor Sea.' Orsino paused, his mouth flattening. 'I had time on my hands and agreed.'

Poppy frowned. 'Paddle? As in canoes? That's harebrained.'

'It seemed like a good idea at the time.' Orsino's lips curved up in a smile that bared his teeth and flashed her a look she couldn't interpret.

'That was my first visit to Timor-Leste, one of the world's poorest countries. But the people couldn't have been friendlier.' He shrugged. 'I stayed and got involved supporting a little hospital that's understaffed and underfunded and does the most fantastic job.

'I promised myself then that instead of just pursuing thrills, each of my trips would raise money for local people in need. The press was already following me and I'd done a couple of awareness-raising stunts for larger charities, but there was something about getting personally involved that appealed. As if I could make a difference.'

His head jerked up and his eyes met hers. 'A god complex, maybe?'

Poppy shook her head, reeling as the import of his words sank in.

All those death-defying adventures of Orsino's were *planned* specifically with the idea of raising funds?

The room dipped and spun. She'd assumed Orsino had simply done what he always had, finding new challenges for purely personal enjoyment. That the charity angle was a later addition—a happy coincidence. Of course it hadn't been. Why hadn't she realised?

How often had he risked his life for others?

She cleared her throat. 'That's a far cry from moving onto a management board.'

Orsino waved his hand. 'Some places had the need but not the on-the-ground help, so I set about discovering how to get that started.'

Poppy stared. 'You started your own charities?'

'I prefer the word *enterprises*. The emphasis is on local people finding long-term solutions for themselves, with a bit of assistance.' When she didn't respond he spread his hands wide. 'It wasn't me alone. I was connected with people who knew what they were doing. I was just a cog in the wheel.'

She looked down at the complex sheets before her.

'Some wheel. There must be scores of *enterprises* here.' No wonder he had a full-time secretary.

Poppy had the weirdest feeling, as if she'd turned around and the man she'd known—surely she *had* known him?— had revealed himself as someone different.

Orsino had always been charming and at ease in any social situation but there'd also been a sense of distance. A feeling he withdrew into himself sometimes, even when faced with an adoring throng.

Or his young, adoring wife.

Her heart stuttered then took up a tattered beat.

He'd always been self-sufficient and selfish. He'd wanted her with him when it suited him, yet turned his back with never a second glance when opportunity for adventure presented itself. And as for him fitting with her work priorities…!

Yet here was proof he felt strongly for others and connected with them in ways she'd never imagined. That he fitted his life around them.

He'd changed.

She banished the wish that he'd changed sooner. There was no going back.

'As I said, many of them are small-scale, to fit local needs.'

Poppy's gaze went to the computer. She returned to the index page and scanned the list of abbreviations. She stopped at one, blinking.

'I know this one. The women's shelter.' It wasn't in some far-flung place but a mere thirty miles from where she grew up. Learning about it had evoked a cavalcade of mixed emotions, primarily regret for the past that couldn't be altered. 'I hosted a fashion show fundraiser for it just two weeks ago.'

Poppy swung round. Instantly he was distracted by the sultry curve of her Cupid's bow mouth, shimmering like ruby satin, and by the waft of tousled curls that trailed loose from her upswept hair.

She was so beautiful. How could he ever get enough of her?

Then he saw the curiosity on her face and cursed himself for letting her into this part of his life.

There were things she didn't need to know. Like the fact he'd thrown himself into more dangerous challenges, like the sea crossing she called harebrained, to fill a void that had cracked wide open the night she betrayed him.

Adventure had always been solace for him in a world devoid of love. For a time he'd almost believed he'd found something different and precious with Poppy.

Until he discovered Poppy's 'love' was fake. That's when

the urge for thrills had turned darker—into a need to dice with death.

Old pain slashed with razor-sharp claws.

'*You* hosted a charity event?'

The woman he'd married had been so focused on her career, following her beloved Mischa's advice to the letter on how to raise her profile, that Orsino had never imagined her working for nothing.

'You're not the only one with a social conscience, Orsino.' Her head angled higher and her bottom lip jutted belligerently, emphasising her natural pout.

Heat roared up, consuming Orsino. For four nights he'd had his fill of her. He'd taken her urgently, hungrily, slowly, tenderly. Every way he'd wanted. And *she'd* wanted, too. His heart crashed against his ribs as he remembered her passion.

For a pulse-beat fear battered him. Fear he'd been wrong to bed her. That it would be too hard to sever the link between them now they were lovers again.

Then logic reasserted itself. This sexual hunger resulted from prolonged abstinence. Once sated he'd move on and not look back.

He leaned forward, brushing the hair from her face, pushing it behind her delicate ear then trailing his finger over the sensitive spot just below her earlobe.

'I'm sorry, Poppy. I shouldn't have spoken like that.'

Her tongue swiped her lip and he almost groaned aloud. That mouth.

'Let me make it up to you.' His hand drifted to her shoulder then down to skim the hard nub of her nipple. He swallowed a sigh of satisfaction as she quivered. He couldn't have stood being the only one affected by desire.

'How will you do that?' Her voice was a throaty purr as he stroked her again.

'However you like.'

'Anything?' Her fine eyebrows arched.

'Anything.'

'In that case…' Poppy rose to her knees and shuffled forward between his legs. One pale hand shoved at his chest and he let himself slump back into the chair. Her other hand touched his belt, dragging it undone before reaching for the button on his jeans.

Her eyes gleamed. The look of a woman who knew her own power. That sensuous mouth curved in a knowing smile as he felt the slow tug of his zip dragging down.

'You're going to kill me,' he whispered, already rock hard.

Her smile widened. 'And we're both going to enjoy every minute of it.'

CHAPTER NINE

IF OPULENCE AND GLAMOUR could sell jewellery then the House of Baudin was onto a winner, Orsino decided.

The long ballroom jutted out from the chateau forming a bridge over the river. The black-and-white floor was a perfect counterpoint to the swirling, wide-skirted ball gowns of another century as dancers glided from one end of the room to the other. Discreet portable lights added to the illumination from hanging pendants and massive candelabras in each window embrasure.

The scene was rich, exotic and glamorous, a taste of luxury in the style of long ago.

At its heart, vibrant in a dress the colour of garnets, was Poppy. She stood out from the rest like the moon surrounded by faded stars.

When she whirled past him on the arm of her blond partner, Orsino's breath snared. Her skin had the lustre of pearls and he caught the fleeting scent of crushed berries on the air.

Avidly he traced the thrust of her breasts, barely restrained by the dress's low décolletage, the perfect slope of her bare shoulders and the delectable curve of her waist. A king's ransom in gold and rubies glittered at her throat and wrists, yet she outshone them easily.

Every man here desired her. He knew it, felt it in their rapt attention. But, he reminded himself, she'd been even sexier last night as she'd seduced him before the fire in the privacy of their shared sitting room.

Heat poured through him and it took a moment to realise the dancing had stopped and the director was giving instructions at the far end of the room.

He shouldn't be here. He should be wrestling with those figures on the computer, but after last night Orsino couldn't settle to work. Last night something had happened. He wasn't sure what, except that he felt *different*.

Because Poppy hadn't scoffed at his work? Because she'd been interested and helpful? No, the difference had more to do with a slip-through-the-fingers sense that *they*, the two of them, had changed.

He shook his head. His imagination was working overtime. That's what came of sitting around, inactive, for so long.

'You're back.' He turned to see a man emerge from the throng of extras and join him on the sidelines. It was the one he'd chatted to on the riverbank.

'You're a hairdresser?' Orsino gestured to the bag of supplies in his hand.

'Stylist, we prefer to be called.' Then he grinned. 'Keeping busy with this scene, too. Most of the models don't have hair long enough to be worn up like they did a few hundred years ago, so we've had to improvise. Your Poppy is the exception.'

Orsino ignored the trickle of warmth across his breastbone at the sound of 'your Poppy'.

'But her hair's down around her shoulders.' Had he missed something?

The other man shrugged. 'Technically, to fit the time period, she should wear it up, too, but what a waste that would be. Besides, Mischa insisted that in this scene she had to look sultry. As if she'd just got out of bed with her lover.'

Orsino stared, watching as Poppy draped herself closer to her partner while the lighting was adjusted again.

'Mischa?' His voice seemed to come from far away.

His companion gave him a curious look. 'The one who

discovered Poppy when she was fifteen. Of course he was a photographer then, not Baudin's creative director, but they've worked together for years.'

Orsino choked down a tide of bile and fury. Mischa and Poppy.

Oh, yes, he knew exactly how close they were.

'I know Mischa.' Did the other guy realise he spoke through gritted teeth? It was a wonder he got the words out, given the swamping fury that blindsided him. 'I hadn't realised he was involved in this project.'

'Involved? He brought it all together. That's how Baudin got Poppy Graham—through Mischa. This series of advertisements is his baby.'

Through a rising red mist Orsino watched Poppy smile up at her partner on the dance floor. He catalogued the man's tall, slim build. His high, Slavic cheekbones and ash-blond hair. Suddenly so much made sense.

Mischa's pet project.

Mischa's model.

Finally Orsino made the connection. The guy with Poppy bore a striking resemblance to the man who'd stolen Orsino's wife: Mischa. Her old 'friend' Mischa, who'd always been jealous of Orsino and hated him for diverting her attention from their work together.

Was the bastard reliving his affair with Poppy vicariously through the male model? Turning it into some twisted fantasy on film he could revisit again and again?

Orsino's breath hissed into lungs that clamped too tight. He fought for breath, his vision tunnelling to nothing as a long-banished image unfurled in his head.

The street outside their London apartment. A cab's lights illuminated parked cars and the murky piles of ice that passed for snow in the city. Orsino heard it crunch under his boots as he stepped off the pavement to cross the road.

Ahead a figure exited the lobby's glass doors, walking at right angles to him. A tall man, his pale hair rumpled.

He shrugged into a jacket and, as he passed under a street-light, Orsino recognised him. Mischa, Poppy's guide and guru in her modelling career.

The glare of light revealed two other things. First, his shirt flopped loose from his trousers, the buttons askew as if he'd been too distracted to dress properly. This, the man whose world view was driven by the need to look perfect!

Second, what appeared to be lipstick smeared across his collar. And another smudge on his cheek.

'Sorry? Did you say something?'

Orsino swallowed the growl vibrating in his throat and fought his way back to the present. The ballroom. The man beside him. Poppy looking impossibly sexy, wrapped in the arms of a stranger who looked like the one man on earth he truly hated.

'Nothing. Nothing at all.'

Orsino needed space, action, movement. Something to *do*. Something to focus on other than the buzz of emotion rippling under his skin like swarming ants.

But he couldn't simply hop in a fast car and drive through the night. His damned faulty eyesight kept him prisoner here.

Watching the filming was the only distraction on offer. If he concentrated hard maybe he'd remember he wasn't supposed to feel anything but lust for Poppy.

It took hours, testing his patience to screaming point. The evening progressed and it grew cold. His bad hand curled into a useless claw at his side, a legacy of the frostbite. A number of extras sneaked tipples from a flask.

Finally it was over: people everywhere, a bustle as equipment was turned off and moved. Cords were rolled up, instructions shouted, weary shoulders slumping as models in rich silks and velvets streamed past.

Orsino stood waiting.

The tall blond who'd been at Poppy's side all night

walked past, resplendent in a colourful officer's uniform of another age. Orsino barely spared him a glance. The dresser responsible for Poppy's jewellery hurried by, clutching a stack of flat leather cases.

The huge room emptied but still she didn't come when the overhead lights were switched off.

It was dark at the far end of the vast ballroom yet he made out movement, the sound of voices.

Orsino headed towards them.

'I didn't, I tell you! You don't know what you're talking about. You're drunk.' He heard the woman's urgent voice from afar.

'Don't lie to me! I saw you with him. You were all over him.' The man's words were a slurred roar of rage.

Orsino quickened his pace.

'It's the part I'm playing. That's all. You know I'd never—'

'Of course you would! You're all the same, teasing and leading a guy on then dumping him.'

There was a blur of movement and Orsino cursed, lengthening his stride and hoping he didn't trip over something in the gloom.

'Ow! You're hurting me. Let me go.' Fear threaded the woman's voice.

The shadows ahead resolved into figures. A man looming over a woman in a shimmery dress, his hand around her wrist as she struggled, her long skirt billowing. And at her side, another woman in a dress he knew to be the colour of dark rubies, her bare shoulders and breasts gleaming in the moonlight from a nearby window.

'Let her go.' It was Poppy who spoke, her voice hard and low, vibrating fierce energy.

'You keep out of this!' The man released the other woman and swung violently towards Poppy. She backed a step, ducked and in a flash of movement somehow tipped the aggressor over her to sprawl on the floor.

Orsino pounded forward, the taste of fear, like hot metal, searing his mouth. He stumbled over something but righted himself and surged forward, fury and adrenaline powering him.

Poppy stepped back, spreading her arms wide as if to protect the other woman. The man staggered to his feet, spewing a stream of vicious threats. Head down, he barrelled towards her.

Orsino launched himself, cannoning into him with a bone-jarring thump that made stars wink and spin behind his eyes and pain hammer through every part of him. Half-healed injuries throbbed anew.

Blood roared in his ears as they grappled. He smelled alcohol and sweat, and the rusty tang of blood. Excruciating pain lanced as fists pummelled and a vicious kick connected with his knee.

Sheer rage kept him going.

This…scum had attacked Poppy.

His fist connected with soft belly and again with a hard jaw in a crunch of bone on bone that blasted his good hand into agony.

Then there was nothing except his ragged breathing and the blood pounding like a jackhammer in his head, throbbing fire through his body with every beat.

He staggered to his feet, his knee barely taking his weight. Soft hands reached for him, running over him as if making sure he was all there.

'My jaw. You've broken my jaw.'

Orsino looked at the man sprawled at his feet. He recognised him—the guy who'd badmouthed Poppy by the river.

A ripple of bloodlust shuddered through Orsino and he surged forward, only to pull up short when Poppy's hold on his arm tightened. She dragged at him with all her weight.

Orsino drew a juddering breath and forced himself to stand back.

'If it was broken you wouldn't be able to talk.' It was Poppy's voice, crisp and unsympathetic.

Orsino swung round to her. His hand trembled as it cupped her face, slipped over the satin perfection of her cheek and brushed the soft richness of her hair.

She looked unharmed.

His heart clenched around a single shaky beat of relief that rose to his throat and shut down his larynx.

He opened his mouth to speak but couldn't. Something welled up inside, like a hot tide, filling him and spilling over.

'Orsino. Are you all right?' Then she was warm against him, hands clutching so hard he winced as pain awoke. The rustle of her dress almost drowned out her little cry, half sob, half gasp, as she lifted his bruised knuckles to her lips.

'You really need to see a doctor.' Poppy worked to keep her voice firm as she dipped the face cloth into warm water and wrung it out.

Her hands were unsteady, she realised. Her bones had turned to water when she'd seen Orsino locked in that writhing, vicious brawl and they still hadn't recovered. How she'd found strength to support him back to their rooms she didn't know.

That he'd managed to limp here defied logic. By rights he should be lying down, waiting for medical attention.

When he'd flown through the air to take down her attacker, fear had held her frozen and disbelieving.

She shook her head. Orsino had fought for her. Disabled as he was he'd thrown himself into danger.

To protect her.

The cloth slipped back into the bowl, her nerveless fingers shaking like silk ribbons before a wind machine.

No one had ever protected her like that.

No one but her mother, whose efforts had been ineffectual against an enraged, drunken brute.

Poppy squeezed her eyes shut, reliving those heart-in-mouth moments when Orsino had put himself between her and danger. When he'd absorbed the blows of a man made unnaturally strong by drink and jealousy.

She knew exactly how powerful drink could make an angry man.

'Poppy? What is it?'

Her eyes snapped open and she saw her hands twined together so hard the knuckles gleamed white.

'Why did you do it?' She whipped round, her full skirt swishing around her legs.

Orsino sat on the edge of the bed wearing only jeans and boots, hair tousled and dark features brooding. Blood oozed from a cut on his collarbone and his lip was swollen. Red marks, soon to be more bruises, marred his body and the hand cradling his plaster cast was bloody.

He'd never looked more devastatingly charismatic, more potently male. Deep, deep inside, something vital melted as her gaze skittered over him.

'What do you mean?' His brows drew together.

'Why did you tackle him?' Her voice wasn't her own. It wobbled uncontrollably, like the trembling that started up in her knees.

Orsino reared back, his eyes widening.

'You can't be serious.'

'Look at you!' Her voice rose despite her effort to keep it even. 'You're still recuperating from being crushed in an *avalanche*! No one thought you'd survive. And now you... you...'

Poppy shook her head, her unbound hair swirling around her in a dark cloud. She couldn't find words because she didn't understand what it was she felt.

Fear for him, yes. Worry that he'd damaged that arm again, or his ribs, or worse still, his eyes. But something else, too. Something so huge and inexplicable she couldn't begin to analyse it. It pressed down on her chest, an immovable weight, and clogged her throat when she tried to swallow. Her head reeled as if she'd been clouted in the head—her and not Orsino.

'I didn't need you to rescue me. I'm not your responsibility, remember?' Her breath shuddered into her lungs. 'It's not as if you're...' She waved a hand in the air.

'Your husband?'

Her eyes snapped to his. Ebony dark, they stripped her to the core. Despite her ball gown she felt as if she was naked before him. Worse, as if he saw the confused, distraught woman she hid inside.

'That's precisely what I am. Your husband.' His eyes narrowed assessingly.

'In name only.'

She watched Orsino's jaw tighten, cords of tension roping his neck.

'You think I'd leave *any* woman to that bastard's mercy?'

Something shifted inside. 'So you'd have done that for any woman.'

'Yes.' He paused. 'But when I saw it was you...' His stare bored into her, igniting heat to counteract the chill that held her body in stasis. Flames licked her belly, her breasts, her heart.

'Yes?'

She didn't want to know. She really didn't want to know. They'd agreed there was no relationship, no future for them. Just sexual pleasure. But some yearning part of her leaned closer.

'When I saw it was you I wanted to kill him.'

CHAPTER TEN

HIS WORDS HUNG in the still air. Orsino couldn't even bring himself to regret giving so much away. Not when her eyes looked like windows to a soul in torment.

Gingerly he lifted his hand and rubbed his collarbone, almost grateful for the hard throb of pain filling his body. But it wasn't enough to distract him from her.

'Poppy?'

He'd stunned her. He read it in her slack jaw and staring eyes. He recalled her sheltered upbringing, her years in a cloistered boarding school for girls that catered to the flowers of Britain's aristocracy. She'd probably never seen so much as a punch thrown in her life, much less real bloodlust.

For that's what he'd felt when that lowlife had lunged at Poppy. He'd wanted to pound the guy's head into the floor so hard he'd never get up again.

Or maybe she was shocked not just at the violence, but at his need to protect *her*.

Slowly Orsino flexed his fingers and pain screamed up his arm.

Poppy wasn't the only one in shock. His visceral response to the sight of her in danger overrode everything he thought he knew about the pair of them.

He told himself he'd react the same way if any woman had been in that situation. It was true, but he knew with a certainty that punched a hole through his belly that he wouldn't have *felt* the same. As if someone had taken a hunting knife to his guts and yanked them from his body.

How could he feel that away about a woman who was going to walk out of his life soon?

He didn't want her as his wife. Not after her betrayal, yet still something bound them. Something more profound than sex.

Suddenly Orsino felt wearier than he had since he'd hauled Michael out of the ice. He slumped, the adrenaline finally wearing off enough for his body to feel the full extent of his pain.

'Orsino!'

She was there beside him, her hands warm and soft on his bare skin. He groaned. How could he feel pain and arousal at the same time?

Dimly he acknowledged either was better than grappling with the conundrum that was Poppy and her place in his world. He'd think about that later. Much later.

'You need a doctor. I'll call one now.'

'No!' His hand closed around her wrist. 'Not tonight. Tomorrow's soon enough. For now I just want to rest.'

'But what if—?'

'Please, Poppy. Don't fuss. I'm bruised and sore but that's all.' His grip loosened, his fingers threading through hers.

Still she looked worried; her teeth sank into her bottom lip and her brow puckered.

'If you want something to do you can help me into bed.' Suddenly he felt a hundred years old, each movement an exercise in exquisite agony. 'I'll even let you share with me.'

He waggled his eyebrows in an approximation of a leer and was rewarded with a huff of laughter. It was the best thing he'd heard all day.

'Not even you could think about sex right now.'

Orsino let his gaze drop to the creamy swell of her breasts above the low neckline of her dress. Was it still called a neckline when it skimmed the plump flesh just a fraction above her nipples?

His mouth twisted in a smile that stretched his bruised lip. He groaned again and was rewarded with a light caress along his neck and shoulder.

'I approve of the dress. Take it off.'

'Soon.' He looked up, surprised. 'But only because the designer would have my hide if I damaged it.'

Ten minutes later Orsino lay naked in bed. Poppy lay beside him, demurely covered in a T-shirt of his that hung down her thighs.

He didn't know whether to be annoyed or thankful that she'd refused to leave him to go upstairs to get her own clothes. But he wouldn't have missed the sight of her in his T-shirt for anything. Plain grey cotton had never looked so alluring.

Yet even dosed with painkillers he didn't have the strength left to do more than wrap her close, revelling in the waft of her breath warm across his chest, the weight of her head on his shoulder and one slim leg tangled with his.

It must be the medication but he felt he could happily stay like this for ever.

'Thank you.' It was a breath of sound in the darkness. 'For what you did. For stopping him.'

'You did quite a job of stopping him yourself.' Orsino refused to dwell on what might have happened. 'That was some move you made. Where did you learn it?'

'Self-defence classes.'

'I'm glad you never had to use what you learned before now.'

His hand drifted over the curve of her waist. But instead of supple softness Poppy was rigid beneath his touch.

She'd been on edge ever since that scene in the ballroom. Despite her quick thinking in dealing with her attacker, she'd worn the glazed look of someone in shock.

His stomach curdled. 'You haven't needed any self-defence moves before, have you?'

The silence stretched into a yawning chasm. Orsino felt her quiver.

'Poppy?' He tried to see her face but she turned into his shoulder, her breathing uneven against his flesh.

'It wouldn't have done much good. I was just a kid. I don't think I'd have been a match for him.'

'Him?' Orsino's grip hardened and he forced himself to relax, lifting his hand to stroke her hair, though his insides roiled in churning frenzy.

A shuddering sigh broke from her.

'My father.'

His belly turned into a lump of frigid metal. 'He beat you?' Orsino could barely form the words. His hand stilled, caught in her long tresses.

'Usually my mother. But if I got in the way…' She shrugged. 'That's why she sent me away to school, to keep me safe. She sold off her jewellery and the last of her inheritance from her parents to fund my boarding school.'

'I—' He swallowed, searching for words that just wouldn't come. He pulled her closer. The rapid thump of her heart revealed how much the memory cost her.

'But why?' He knew there were violent men in the world. Hell, he'd helped establish shelters for their victims. Yet he couldn't get his head around the fact Poppy was a victim, too.

'Because he was a vicious bully?' Shakily she laughed, the wretched sound tearing strips from his heart.

'My mother always made excuses, saying, "If only you'd known him in the old days". Apparently things changed when he lost the family money through bad investments. He kept the estate, just, but not the money. That's when he took to drink. And when he drank he got angry and took it out on her.'

'And you.' His body vibrated in a surge of furious energy that had no outlet. The thought of her defenceless and battered skewered him with a razor-sharp blade.

'Only a couple of times.'

'A couple of times too many.'

'Oh, Orsino.' He felt the spill of dampness from her lashes like a brand on his skin.

He wasn't good with tears. He'd never been adept at dealing with feelings or offering comfort. He'd tried when her mother died but Poppy had turned away, closing in on herself, rejecting him. An ice-cold hand squeezed his innards at the memory.

Clumsily Orsino patted at her head, wishing he could ease the hurt he felt in her tightly held body.

'Is that why you took up modelling so young?' Given her intelligence he'd been surprised she hadn't finished school.

She nodded against his shoulder. 'I wanted to be independent as soon as I could.' Her voice was husky with the tears she held in check. 'That was my goal from as early as I could remember. Earn money to make a new home for myself and my mother. Away from him.'

'But she stayed with him.'

'She loved him. Despite it all, she still cared. But she promised me...'

'What?' Orsino bent his head to hear. Poppy's voice was a mere drift of sound.

'She promised that one day she'd leave him. When I broke into the big time and had enough to support her. We had such plans.' Her voice wobbled with pain. 'The fun we'd have together. Just simple things, you know, but special to us. Those dreams kept me going. I'd always promised myself I'd make it up to her for all she'd been through.'

Orsino's heart dived at the throb of anguish in her scratchy voice.

'But she didn't leave him,' Orsino said. Poppy had already been a rising star when he'd met her, yet she'd lived alone.

'No. He was diagnosed with a terminal illness just when I thought I'd convinced her to come away. She stayed—said he needed her.' The pain and incredulity in Poppy's voice told their own tale.

Orsino knew the rest. Her father had died just before their whirlwind wedding then in a brutal blow Poppy's mother had outlived her husband by a mere few months.

He digested what Poppy had just shared.

He'd known she was distraught when her mother died. That had been obvious even to a man who'd never known a parent's love, whose mother was a vague memory and whose father was too caught up in business and his own pleasure to connect with his children.

Poppy's grief had been beyond his understanding, though he'd tried. How he'd tried.

Now, discovering this bond between mother and daughter made her anguish more understandable. He wished he'd tried even harder.

If she'd set her heart on helping her mother how difficult it must have been to face her sudden death—all those dreams destroyed.

He smoothed Poppy's back in long strokes with a hand that trembled. If he'd been able to comfort her better when she lost her mother would she have shunned him as she had?

Would she have sought solace in the arms of another man? A pain that had no physical explanation punctured his chest.

Had his own inadequacy pushed her away?

It went against everything Orsino believed about himself even to consider it. Yet he couldn't dislodge the kernel of disturbing thought from his brain.

Orsino was used to thinking himself invincible. But those hours facing death in the ice had torn away that comfortable lie. He was as human as the next man.

Was he also fatally flawed?

From the age of seven Orsino had hidden what passed for his feelings behind a facade of charm and smiles. No, it had been earlier than that. Had he ever felt secure enough, loved enough, to be honest about emotions?

His features screwed up in a grimace.

What was the point of revisiting the past? It was done and dusted, the damage too late to fix.

Yet he had to know more.

'You never told me. We were married but you never said a word.' Another case of her shutting him out?

'We were married for just four months! Besides, we didn't talk about our families. I never met most of yours. Just Lucca.'

'We're not a close family.' Now there was an under-statement.

'Anyway, my father was dead. There didn't seem any point talking about it.'

Her words didn't ring true. Once Orsino might have been convinced, but he'd spent the past five years learning to work with people, often people under incredible stress. He'd learned a little about reading emotion.

'No point telling your husband how badly you were hurting?' He'd bet everything he had she only shared now because the shock of tonight's attack had thrown her off balance.

Poppy stiffened under his slow caress. He felt her blink against his skin.

'There never seemed to be a right moment to dredge up the past. And what good would it have done?'

Orsino thought about that, remembering their volatile courtship. Neither had been hanging out for a life partner. But they'd been swept off their feet in a rush of passion that had them alternately insatiable in each other's arms and backing off, wary of the intensity of what they felt.

At least in his case it had been like that. Till he'd realised he wanted Poppy not just in his bed but in his life and went after her, determined not to let her slip through his fingers.

A quick marriage had been his way of ensuring she was his. He'd needed her so badly even his cynicism about marriage and families had crumbled when it meant having Poppy.

Fat lot of good that had done him when she decided to betray him with Mischa.

Mischa. Orsino gritted his teeth.

No. Not now. Mischa's involvement in this advertising project was for later.

Orsino's 'simple' arrangement with Poppy—sex with no ties and no regrets—was becoming far more complex than he'd thought possible.

Mischa and the outside world could wait.

'Or maybe you had no intention of ever letting me into that part of your life.' He'd be damned if he shouldered all the guilt for what had gone wrong.

He'd tried to be there for her when her mother died but Poppy had turned her back in spectacular fashion. Who could blame him for leaving on his climbing trip when she'd virtually shoved him out the door?

Poppy made to roll away but his grip tightened.

'Why, Poppy? Didn't I deserve your trust?' Orsino's voice grated against something raw inside. Something he now realised had never healed, not since the day he'd come home to find she'd been with another man.

Part of him, the macho take-it-on-the-chin-and-hide-your-feelings part, writhed and screamed that he should even ask. The other part, too long silent, had to know, even if it gutted him.

Poppy's hand splayed wide on his chest and Orsino closed his eyes, revelling in the magic of her touch even now, when he felt half dead.

'Would you have wanted to know?' she asked finally.

'Of course!' How could she even ask?

'There's no *of course* about it. You never talked about feelings, Orsino. You said you needed me. That you *wanted* me. That life would be so good together. But I was never sure…'

'What?' He moved, trying to see her face in the gloom, but she tilted her head away.

'It doesn't matter. Go to sleep. You need rest.'

Orsino ground his teeth. Was there ever a more infuriating woman? The feel of her body against his was like a glimpse of paradise and the tentative truce they'd declared should have made life easy, yet she insisted on being difficult. Did she do it deliberately?

'You really think I'm going to sleep now you've left me hanging like that? Spit it out. What weren't you sure about?'

'As if you don't know.' Her breath shuddered against his skin. 'I never knew whether you loved me.' Her voice was defiant, yet behind the bravado he heard it tremble.

Orsino groped for a response, but his brain was too busy trying and failing to process what she'd said.

She'd thought he hadn't loved her?

Why would he *marry* her if he hadn't loved her?

He'd had women chasing him since his teens. Women who wanted a chunk of the Chatsfield family fortune, or a celebrity husband who could provide a luxury lifestyle to boot.

Surely the fact he'd chosen Poppy, instead of one of the hundreds of others, was proof enough!

'The sex was fantastic, of course, but there was always a part of you closed off from everyone else. Behind the charisma and the charm was someone I knew I couldn't reach.'

She paused and he wondered dully what had possessed him to ask for the truth.

Hadn't he known probing the past was a mistake?

'Like your trips away.'

'What about them?' Impatience tinged his tone. Those

climbing trips had been part of his life since his teens. They had kept him sane and functioning in a dysfunctional family, in a society where everyone wanted something and nothing seemed to have real value or depth.

'I don't know,' she admitted. 'But they were important to you and whenever I asked about them you clammed up. You didn't want me involved.'

Great! According to her he'd screwed up their marriage because he'd continued to enjoy outdoor treks she hadn't a hope of keeping up with. And because he hadn't said 'I love you' enough.

Orsino's mouth flattened.

Typical of her to blame him when the reason for their marriage crashing and burning was her lust for another man. He opened his mouth to give her a blast but his brain seemed to have no control over his tongue.

'I'm sorry you felt that way, Poppy.'

It was true. Despite the anguish she'd caused, regret seeped through him.

He'd had to be resilient and self-sufficient from an early age and his predilection for extreme sports had honed his ability for intense personal focus.

Had he really shut her out by clinging to what had been his lifeline—his escapes to the wilderness?

It seemed impossible. Yet he'd learned in the past years that people and their needs were anything but simple.

Against his shoulder she nodded, sliding her long, soft hair in a caress across his skin. 'It's over, Orsino. It doesn't matter. I don't even know why we're discussing it. There's no going back.'

She took the words out of his mouth.

He told himself that was good. She wasn't expecting this affair to go anywhere once it reached its natural conclusion.

It was only much later, when the sound of Poppy's even breathing told him she'd finally fallen asleep, that he found himself wondering.

In the days when it had still been true, had he ever told Poppy he loved her?

Or, it struck him suddenly, had he, the man renowned for reckless courage, been too scared?

CHAPTER ELEVEN

THE WHOOSHING ROAR of the burners made conversation impossible but Poppy didn't mind. From here, suspended high above fields and forests, she watched the peach-gold dawn glaze the landscape. Long shadows stretched inky blue as if retreating from the light. Pale patches of frost hadn't yet melted.

Threads of mist clung to the river as it meandered around a bluff topped by a moated fairytale castle that bristled with round towers.

Below was an ancient town with steeply tiled roofs and narrow streets. Poppy craned her neck over the edge of the basket in fascination.

The pilot switched off the blast of heat firing the hot air balloon and in the blissful silence she heard the cry of a lone bird.

'It's nothing like being in a plane.' She felt her smile spread across her features. 'This is so…real. Looking out a plane window it all seems so far away. But this—I can almost smell the earth and the wood smoke.'

Orsino moved behind her, his big frame solid at her back. She leaned into him, luxuriating in his nearness. A secret smile curved her lips as his hand rubbed her arm. Even through the heavy coat his touch was magic.

'Totally different,' he murmured. 'I'm glad you like it.'

'How could I not?' She swung around. 'It's glorious.'

He didn't smile back, but something that looked like

pleasure lurked at the corner of his mouth and a long dimple grooved his cheek. With his dark, unshaven jaw and wind-tousled hair, and the early sun highlighting the tiny creases beside his eyes, he looked exactly what he was: an adventurer. Like the highwaymen and pirates she'd fantasised about in her girlish dreams.

Poppy's heart careered as her eyes met his and she saw a glow of warmth.

'Not everyone appreciates the solitary splendour of it. Some prefer bright lights, glamour and bustle.'

'Is that what you think of me?' Their focus had always been on the present, never what had gone before.

Orsino shrugged. 'We met in the city. You lived and worked there the whole time I knew you.' Poppy swallowed, wondering why his use of the past tense saddened her. 'We were always going out to clubs or opening nights.'

Poppy nodded. Their marriage had been a whirl of activity. Until it had fallen apart. Who'd have guessed they could talk so amicably now?

She kept her voice low, aware they weren't alone. 'I was brought up in the country. I loved getting up as the sun rose to go for a long ride.' Until her father sold her old pony, trying to pay debts.

'What else did you enjoy?'

Poppy turned and looked at the slowly drifting landscape. In the distance she saw their chateau straddling the river, surrounded by its geometrically patterned gardens and the forest beyond. The scene's delicate beauty stole her breath.

'Would you believe, fishing?' It had been so long, she'd almost forgotten. 'Our neighbour was an expert. I used to tag along.' Those were the days she found any excuse to get out of the house and away from her father.

'Somehow I can't imagine you in waders.' Orsino's breath breezed the back of her neck and she shivered, pulling her warm jacket closer.

'You'd be surprised.' She smiled. 'The first time I actually hooked a fish I was so stunned I stumbled and ended up drenched from head to toe.'

Orsino chuckled. 'I'd never picked you for a lover of the great outdoors.' He paused and when he spoke again his voice was sober. 'Maybe I should have brought you somewhere like this five years ago. I love the peace up here. It's like climbing. Just you in the vast wilderness. It's…cathartic, pitting yourself against nature. There's something clean and real about it. No room for falsehood or empty words. No pretence. What you see is what you get, however harsh.'

Poppy swivelled around but it was hard to read his face. He'd donned his dark glasses as the sun rose and the light intensified. Every instinct clamoured that here was something absolutely vital to Orsino. These adventures weren't just fun for him. They were *necessary.*

'I would have liked that.' Poppy swallowed, wondering how different things would have been if he'd shared some of this with her years ago. 'I didn't know you were a balloonist.'

Orsino turned and gestured to the lanky Frenchman piloting them. 'Thierry is the balloonist. I was always just along for the ride.'

'I'm glad you admit it at last, Orsino,' Thierry said in accented English, his smile flashing. 'That trip across South America you were pure baggage, except when we landed and you got to pose for the cameras.'

Orsino laughed, the sound far too appealing, and the mood lightened.

Thierry poured mugs of rich hot chocolate from a large thermos and passed them around. Poppy wrapped gloved hands around hers and inhaled the fragrant steam.

She looked from one man to the other, reading the camaraderie and genuine respect behind their banter as they relived past trips with anecdotes that grew more and more outrageous. 'You two shared a balloon for *weeks*?'

'It was for charity, you understand, and Orsino brought

the media attention.' Thierry winked. 'I suppose he was useful in his own way, but if I do something like that again, perhaps you'd consider coming with me instead, Mademoiselle Graham.'

'Don't even think about it,' Orsino drawled. 'Try your fabled charm elsewhere, Thierry. She's taken.'

Poppy's eyes bulged. *Taken?* Did Orsino realise that implied longevity in a relationship that was due to end soon? Or was it part of his joking rivalry with his friend?

The roar of the burners stopped further conversation and Poppy turned to lean against the basket and gaze at the view.

She was glad she'd agreed to come with Orsino today on her day off.

Maybe it was the thrill of being up here, or perhaps because they'd reached some sort of understanding, but she knew what he meant about a sense of peace. She felt like she'd left her troubles down on the ground.

Ever since agreeing to Orsino's demand that he stay with her, doubts had racked her about the wisdom of getting too close. About getting hurt again.

But here she felt exhilaration and pleasure. She understood why he loved this. Man against the elements. Adventure and, yes, peace.

She sipped her hot chocolate, feeling its warmth trace down her insides.

As it did an outrageous thought struck her. She almost choked on her drink.

Orsino wasn't just taking her on a pleasant outing. He was sharing his private world. The world he'd barred her from all those years ago.

She swung round to find him braced against the other side of the basket, his gaze fixed on her. A frisson of excitement tiptoed over her nape and down her backbone.

Ballooning was part of his world of challenge and outdoor adventure. Yet here he was, not only sharing the experience but introducing her to one of his friends.

What had changed?

Poppy read the tension in his straight shoulders and wondered with a crazy skip of her pulse why he chose to share now. And why it mattered so much that he did.

An hour later, after smiling farewells to Thierry, the driver Orsino had organised delivered them to a small *manoir*, nestled in private parkland. It was the property of absent friends, Orsino explained.

Now he and Poppy enjoyed a champagne brunch in a sun-drenched conservatory. The friendly housekeeper who'd served had left them to their privacy.

Poppy found herself chuckling over another of Orsino's unlikely stories, this one about Thierry, a disabled hot air balloon and an enormous python somewhere over the Amazon. Wiping tears of laughter from her eyes, she realised she hadn't enjoyed herself so much in weeks.

No, she realised abruptly. Months.

Her smile faded. It couldn't be years, could it?

That was impossible. She'd been happy pursuing her career goals. Hard work brought its rewards, like financial security—so important to her after her father's profligacy had turned him sour and destroyed their family. Work gave her independence. Success meant she'd never have to rely on anyone, especially a man, the way her mother had.

But looking back on those years since Orsino, Poppy realised she'd been so busy building her career she'd done precious little else. At the back of her mind was always the fear that if she failed she'd lose that precious control over her life. She'd taken on job after demanding job, forever focused on the next career goal.

When was the last time she'd taken time out to laugh with a friend?

And since when did Orsino qualify as a friend?

She raised her crystal flute and swallowed vintage champagne, letting it trickle down her throat. It was a decadent delight in her life of perpetual diet consciousness.

'Poppy? What is it?'

She looked up through veiling lashes, shocked at how the hint of concern in Orsino's voice evoked feelings she should have buried ages ago. Tiny furrows pleated his tanned forehead. The scar above his eye was paler now, less confronting.

'Nothing at all.' She pinned a smile on her features.

Since that night when Orsino had put himself between her and danger, she'd been puzzling over the sense that he *cared*.

It would drive her mad trying to fathom what was going on between them.

Their short-term, no-holds-barred sexual relationship with no future had veered into something fragile and new. She refused to analyse it.

All she knew was that with Orsino she felt more alive, more authentically herself, than she had in ages.

And now, having him share these glimpses of his life with her...

'You asked about my childhood before,' she said impulsively. 'How about you? What was your favourite thing as a child?'

'Sports days,' he said promptly. 'I liked winning.'

Poppy grinned. Why didn't that surprise her? The combination of athleticism and challenge would have suited Orsino to a T.

'What about earlier? What do you remember when you were little?' She couldn't resist the opportunity to probe. Orsino was rarely so talkative.

He shrugged. 'Hot drinks and adventure stories in bed. At boarding school they gave us younger ones cocoa before lights out.'

'You must have been young.' It didn't sound like her school.

'Lucca and I boarded from the age of seven.'

So young! Poppy had been a teenager when she'd boarded.

'Don't look so horrified.' Orsino swallowed the last of his wine and put his glass down. 'Boarding school was everything I needed back then.'

'Everything?'

He snagged the wine bottle and leaned across, topping up her glass before she thought to protest. Then he refilled his own before turning back to her.

'You think I missed home?' His mouth twisted bitterly and sadness snaked through her. Poppy couldn't remember caring for her father, but she'd loved her mother and missed her warm cuddles when she went away to school. Hadn't Orsino felt the same?

'My father sent us away the week after my mother abandoned us.' Orsino reached out and twisted the stem of his wineglass on the white linen cloth. 'We were too much of a handful to stay home.'

'What, all of you?' She knew he had older siblings.

'Maybe he blamed us twins.' Orsino shrugged heavily as if shedding a burden. 'Our mother was apparently a vivacious, gracious woman, full of joy and life. But after delivering Lucca and me she slumped into severe postnatal depression. She withdrew from everyone and never recovered. In the circumstances you'd think it foolhardy of our parents to have another child after us, but eventually they did.'

He lifted his glass and took a long swallow. 'When Cara was born our mother's depression got worse. She just left one day and we've never heard from her since.'

Poppy gaped. She'd heard that Orsino's mother wasn't around but she'd never imagined this. 'But didn't she—?'

'There was no more contact.' His mouth was grim. 'Clearly she didn't want to be found. I tried myself some time ago, but the trail had gone cold years before. Wherever she is, alive or dead, we'll never know.'

Poppy leaned forward and covered his hand with hers, her heart contracting at his bitterness and the pain she sensed behind that stern expression. 'I'm so sorry, Orsino.'

What had it been like, believing your father blamed you for the loss of your mother? That's what Orsino implied and the notion horrified her. They'd been tiny, innocent children!

'Your father must have been distraught.'

'Must he?' Orsino's hand clenched on the table beneath hers. She felt the vibrating tension in each sinew. 'I suspect he was busy with other…diversions. Whatever the case, he wasn't interested in us. He wasn't the sort of father to fly kites or kick a football with his sons.'

Orsino's hand turned, his long fingers threading between hers. 'Our mother rejected us from the day we were born. She rarely spent time with us so I have few memories of her. At least she had a reason, given her depression. But our father? He left it to staff and our older siblings to bring us up. Antonio and Lucilla tried their best but they were only teenagers themselves. As soon as our mother walked he packed us off.'

'I'm sorry.' The words were inadequate but they were all she could manage.

How could she not have known this? What did it say about their brief marriage that this was new to her? The thought of those two little boys, alone and unloved, scraped at something raw and painful inside.

'Don't be sorry.' Orsino drew her hand to his mouth and pressed a kiss to her fingers. He turned her hand over and laved the sensitive skin of her wrist till she shivered and delicious excitement rippled through her.

'School was a relief. It had rules and structure and routine that we'd never had before. And no matter how fierce some of the teachers were, I always knew they'd notice if I disappeared.'

Poppy blinked at that devastating assessment.

Orsino believed his father hadn't noticed his absence? What sort of man *was* Gene Chatsfield? She'd give a lot to tell him just what she thought of a man who abandoned his children.

'Are you and your father closer now?' He hadn't been at their wedding, but as they'd eloped with no family or fanfare, that meant nothing.

Orsino's laugh was harsh. 'You're kidding. He's too busy with his precious new woman and his all-important business to bother with anything so mundane. Though I did hear from him last month. Not him personally, of course, but via his new CEO. He wants me to be the face of Chatsfield Enterprises. Something about my philanthropic work being good PR for the company.'

Poppy reached out her free hand and palmed his cheek, wishing she could smooth away the hurt Orsino still carried deep inside. That scar on his forehead would heal and silver. What about the scars he carried internally?

'We're neither of us lucky with our fathers, are we?' His smile was lopsided.

'But what doesn't destroy us makes us stronger,' she reminded him.

Orsino reached up and removed his sun glasses. His heavy-lidded eyes scrutinised her with an intensity that should have scared her. Instead she met his stare, marvelling at the man she'd uncovered. The man who'd overcome neglect and rejection to grow strong and decent, a champion for others, a man who, despite his surface bravado, cared deeply.

Orsino Chatsfield, her husband, was a far more complex man than she'd ever imagined.

It terrified her how much she cared.

'You're absolutely right.' He lifted her hand to his mouth again and kissed her with a lingering eroticism that made her stomach shimmy and her lips part greedily. If they weren't in someone else's house, in a room that was three sides glass...

He pressed her palm to his rock-hard thigh and Poppy knew she wasn't the only one feeling desire.

Orsino smiled slowly. He reached for her glass, tilting it to her lips. She opened for him, letting the crisp, perfect wine tingle like a promise down her throat.

Orsino watched her swallow and heat flooded her at the gravity, the exquisite focus, of his gaze, as if he didn't miss anything, from the tiny freckle beside her mouth to the way her nipples budded and swelled. Or the fact it was him she wanted to taste, not mere wine.

'Soon, Poppy. I promise.' His smile was only half tamed. He sighed. 'But first we should try to do justice to Heloise's efforts. I know she spent hours preparing this.' He gestured to the barely touched delicacies before them.

Fire scorched Poppy's cheeks as she realised the hunger consuming her had nothing to do with food. Confusion battered her. How could that be? Wasn't her need for him supposed to reduce, not increase, after their time together?

Orsino's hand was gentle as it grazed her cheek.

Then, finally, she registered the glaze of heat in Orsino's eyes. It warred with the slashing grim lines around his mouth that spoke of fierce control.

Their eyes locked and something passed between them.

Poppy sagged back in her seat. Maybe after all, he understood her confusion and fear.

Poppy lay naked against him, her hair lush waves across his chest, her warm breath hazing his chest.

That they'd ended up naked was a miracle. It was a wonder they'd even made it to bed, so frantic had they been for each other. There were clothes strewn from the tower's front door all the way up here to the bedroom.

And still he wanted her.

More. Ever more.

Bad enough that he craved her luscious body as much now as on the first night he'd met her. Even more frightening was the way he craved her smiles, her approval, even, God help him, her sympathy.

When he'd told her about his childhood she'd looked as if she wanted to go after his father with a shotgun. And instead of being furious with himself for spilling secrets he'd never shared, he'd felt ridiculous pleasure at her reaction.

He didn't want her to feel sorry for him, but the way she'd *understood* had healed a little of the ancient pain he'd carried so long.

How was that even possible?

What doesn't destroy us makes us stronger.

Poppy had said it, but it had been Orsino's lifelong motto. How had she known?

Because, he suddenly realised with excruciating clarity, that's what she'd done, too. Push the hurt aside, throw yourself into the next challenge. Ignore the pain and get on with life. They both operated the same way.

Another thing they had in common.

Orsino scrubbed a hand across his jaw, horrified at the direction of his thoughts.

He'd been duped once into thinking he and Poppy shared something stronger than sex. He'd opened himself up to her and she'd carved out his heart and left a jagged hole where it had been.

He needed to remember that, not let himself be seduced by the need to connect to her again.

That's what he'd been doing, wasn't it? Today he'd taken her away from her world of airbrushed perfection and image and glamour and let her into his. He'd shared his past, introduced her to one of his best friends.

Why? Did he really think she cared about anything but her own priorities?

The trouble was he did. He'd begun to suspect Poppy was more than the cold-hearted bitch of his memory.

Orsino shut his eyes, his breath juddering through his lungs as he realised how far he'd strayed from his plan of pleasure and retribution into the quicksands of emotional entanglement.

'Orsino? What is it?' Her voice was soft and delicious with that hint of concern. Chagrin slammed into him as he realised how much he wanted to hear that in her voice—hear that she cared.

Scalding anger bubbled.

It was time to rip away the rose-tinted glasses and face what really lay between them. What he'd been too proud and too cowardly to face. He'd avoided it too long.

'So tell me about Mischa. You didn't mention he's involved in this project.' Orsino paused, feeling the tension ripple through her. 'Does he know we're sharing a bed again or doesn't he have exclusive rights?'

Poppy felt as if Orsino had plunged a knife into her stomach then twisted it hard for good measure.

She reared back, needing distance, needing to see his face, but arms of steel clamped her to him. Her heart pounded as bile rose in her throat.

How could he ask that? Especially after this morning—after they'd shared so much?

She couldn't ever remember feeling as attuned to Orsino as she had today, laughing at his stories, feeling his pain as he'd talked of his past.

Had it been an illusion? Some complicated trickery on his part to make her even more vulnerable to him?

Desperately she struggled for release. Orsino's hot, slick skin slid against hers as she writhed and a flicker of sensual awareness flared into life, making her still instantly.

Gulping, she dragged in a sobbing breath of frustration and despair, inhaling as she did the earthy smell of male heat and sex.

Poppy shuddered. She'd never felt so trapped. Not just

by Orsino's uncompromising strength, but by her body and mind.

'I have no idea what Mischa knows.' Even to her own ears she sounded defeated.

'I find that very hard to believe.' Orsino's voice rumbled up from deep in his chest. She felt the words as he locked her to him.

'Frankly, Orsino, I don't care what you believe.'

It was a lie. She cared too much. This interlude at the chateau had reawakened all those feelings for him she'd thought she'd banished. And more.

How could she feel more? She blinked and bit her lip so hard she tasted the salt tang of blood.

'You didn't tell me he was involved in this project. That he'd organised it.'

'How was that relevant? I don't remember you asking for details when you had me summoned to your hospital bed. Or when you blackmailed me into bringing you here.' She breathed deep and tried to settle her ragged pulse. 'I don't remember you being so choosy then.'

'So you're saying he doesn't mind sharing you with another man?'

Poppy told herself it wasn't hurt she heard in Orsino's voice. 'I'm saying Mischa has no right to care who I sleep with.'

'So you and he aren't together any more? You got this job without his influence?'

Poppy hiccupped on rising hysteria. If only Orsino knew. But of course he'd never believe the truth.

She and Mischa had never been together in the sense Orsino meant. Though familiar, coruscating guilt sideswiped her as she thought of how perilously close they'd come to it. How close she'd let Mischa.

She remembered his hands on her breasts, his mouth on hers and that sudden jerk of sanity in a mind clouded by grief and alcohol. The instant certainty that it wasn't

Mischa she needed but her husband, Orsino, who'd left hours before on one of his precious climbing trips.

Poppy gagged, nausea rising in an unstoppable wave. She shoved at Orsino's ribs and miraculously he let her go.

In a flurry of movement she was off the bed and into the bathroom. Hands braced on either side of the basin, she hung her head. Her body shook, her legs barely able to support her as she fought the need to lose her brunch.

With a few cruelly aimed words Orsino had made her feel like a cheap tart. He'd undercut everything good they'd shared these past weeks—the understanding, the empathy and what she'd thought was budding respect.

Great racking sobs rose in her chest and she forced them down, the pain exquisite as she fought for breath.

Large hands drew the hair back from her face then a strong arm wrapped around her middle, drawing her back against Orsino's heat, holding her steady when her legs would have given way.

Stunned, Poppy stared into the mirror. Orsino looked as bad as she felt. His face was drawn, strain etching lines around his eyes. His mouth was a tight line of pain, as if he hurt as much as she did.

'Why?' Her voice cracked. 'Why did you have to—?'

'Because I can't let it go. I can't forget.'

Sweet pain pierced her at his words. She should want him to forget their past so they could both move on. But she could no more let go than he could.

'Mischa and I never—'

'You're not going to try rewriting history, are you?' Poppy felt Orsino tense behind her, his hold biting into her, his bitter tone harsh in her ears.

The truth died in her throat. The man who'd just accused her of juggling two lovers wasn't ready to hear it, even if the pain in his face gave her hope that at some level he cared.

Despair and regret welled. There was no way out.

'Mischa and I haven't worked together since that night

in London. There is no *relationship*.' Poppy almost choked on the words, remembering how sick with guilt and regret she'd felt that night. Sick enough to turn her back on her friend and mentor, the man who'd stood by her through the early years of her career. The man who'd been there for her when Orsino hadn't. But working with him again had been beyond her. Orsino's pain and her wrecked marriage lay between them. And her guilt.

'And now?' Orsino's hands slid to her waist. In the mirror his hold looked possessive.

Poppy blinked and told herself she imagined it.

'This work for Baudin was too good an opportunity to refuse. When the contract's up I'll be financially secure for life.' It was what she'd worked for since she was fifteen. 'Besides, Mischa's not hands-on with this.' She didn't add that it had taken her a year to agree.

She tilted her chin up and caught a flash of something in Orsino's eyes that made her tremble.

'Good.' He tilted his head forward till his lips grazed her ear. 'Because if I ever catch him *hands-on* with you again I'll rip his head off.'

Orsino's barely repressed violence stunned her almost as much as his jealousy.

But at some blood-deep level, his primal possessiveness appealed in a way she'd never thought possible. She was no man's possession. It went against everything she believed and wanted. It was what had made women like her mother weak.

Yet Orsino's words, his proprietorial hold and the fierce glint in his eyes were shockingly exciting.

If only he'd cared so much five years ago.

'This isn't over between us, Poppy.' One callused hand cupped her breast. She watched, mesmerised, as tanned flesh closed over pale and her body jangled into sensual overload. 'Until it is—' he plucked at her nipple and desire shuddered through her '—I refuse to share.'

His other hand slid down, arrowing between her thighs and a jolt of pleasure stiffened her whole body.

His fingers moved and she was melting, eager for more. She'd never needed him so wantonly, so desperately.

Orsino's other hand left her breast. He tipped her chin till their eyes locked in the mirror. 'I'm going to make love to you,' he growled in a voice that thrummed across her quivering flesh. 'And you're going to watch.'

He pushed her quivering legs apart and bent his knees till the blunt head of his erection probed her. Then, eyes locked with hers, he surged high and hard with such sure force it felt like he touched her heart.

Her fingers clawed the vanity unit as the world began to dissolve.

'I want you to remember with every…single…thrust,' he panted, 'that it's *me* making love to you. Understand?'

Pleasure spiralled and something more, something so profound she had no name for it.

Seconds later, as his pounding thrusts took them both to impossibly perfect climax, it was to the hoarse sound of his name on her lips, and the sight of his dark gaze melded with hers.

CHAPTER TWELVE

'ORSINO!' A GOVERNMENT MINISTER with whom he'd once shared a podium spoke. 'You're looking much better than I expected. I read terrible things in the newspapers about your accident.'

'As you can see, the reports were exaggerated.' He looked around his acquaintances, Parisian A-listers who'd arrived at the floodlit chateau for the lavish party to launch Baudin's latest designs.

'But your eye!' One of the women leaned forward, arm outstretched as if to touch the scar that jagged down his forehead. Her opulent damask rose scent drenched him, making him realise how much he preferred the fresh tang of wild berries.

Instead of shifting away he drew on a smile. She was one of the most recent benefactors to a program that combined saving endangered wildlife with providing jobs and education for villagers in Borneo.

'What? You don't like the scar? There I was hoping it gave me an attractively intriguing air.'

One of the men snorted, drawing his wife close. 'As if you need that.'

Orsino shrugged, cataloguing the avid female interest from the circle around him.

He wished he felt a spark of attraction for one of these women. They were beautiful, some talented and successful, all poised and charming. Yet not one stirred a ripple in his soul.

Because they're not Poppy.

His smile became fixed as his jaw locked.

What he felt for Poppy, the fact that he felt anything other than animal lust for the woman who'd betrayed him, was driving him quietly insane.

He felt mired deep, the link that bound him to her no longer a thread of connection but a web that trapped him however he tried to break away. Even now he missed her and she'd only gone on ahead to dress with the other models for the preparty photos.

'So tell us.' One of the men spoke. 'What's the next big expedition?'

Orsino parried their questions with half a mind, not committing himself.

His bruises and damaged ribs had healed and his fractured arm was on the mend. He'd ditched the walking stick and with luck and care his eyes would heal. Already his vision was clearer. But one hand still closed up in the cold— a legacy of frostbite.

Whether he could climb again had yet to be tested.

He waited for frustration to consume him, fear that his greatest joy could be denied him.

Instead the thought filling his head was that with the shoot ending he had no reason to stay with Poppy.

If he couldn't climb he'd find some other challenge. But deep in his soul lurked the disturbing thought that there was no challenge in the world to match the thrill of being with Poppy, watching her delight in new experiences like sailing above the workaday world in a hot air balloon.

Or watching her brow knit as she deciphered his scrawl and entered notations on a spreadsheet, all the while peppering him with questions about why and how a particular enterprise was run.

Or seeing her come apart in his arms, the sound of his name on her lips.

How could he feel so much for a woman he couldn't trust?

'Orsino?' A hand touched his arm and he looked down, disappointment flaring as he recognised a beautiful brunette he'd spoken to earlier. 'It's time to go in.'

He nodded and joined the crowd heading to the red carpet that led across the arched bridge to the chateau. Floodlit against the inky night it was a fantasy of pure white stone and romantic towers. Flambeaux set along either side of the bridge recalled an earlier age, but the women posing for press photographs on the red carpet were absolutely contemporary.

One, with blond hair and a dress of ice green, he recognised as the model whose drunken boyfriend had caused such a scene. The other...

Orsino's feet welded to the cobblestones as she turned, her rich dark red hair cascading around a face as pale and luminous as moonlight.

Something clawed at his throat as Poppy smiled for the media. The sight of her undid something in his chest, like a long spool unwinding.

Her dress was the colour of wild violets, the purple so dark it looked black till she moved and the light caught. It clung lovingly to each superb inch. Full-length with long, fitted sleeves, it had a deep V neckline at the back and at the front, where it plunged low between her breasts.

His breath stalled and he waited for the fabric to slide aside, revealing one perfect, rose-tipped breast. But by some designer magic he didn't understand, the dress stayed in place, barely.

Around her throat wound a choker of amethysts and pink diamonds. A single, gem-studded strand fell down between her breasts, drawing the eye to all that creamy skin. More stones glittered at her wrists and ears.

She laughed and something dived inside him, arrowing to the very centre of his being.

How was he going to walk away tomorrow, now the shoot, and their deal, was over?

The first time he'd left her had nearly killed him. How could he do it a second time?

Behind the cameras light glinted on pale blond hair. The man wore a dinner suit like the rest of the guests but walked with a lanky stride that unlocked bitter memory. He made a beeline for Poppy.

Mischa.

Orsino felt rage roar to life as Poppy's *old friend* descended on the models, arms wide, kissing their cheeks.

His hands clenched as Mischa touched Poppy's shoulder, leaning close. Poppy smiled back, angling her head for the cameras and a cold, hard weight dropped like a stone in Orsino's gut.

He strode forward then slammed to a halt, eyes narrowing as he saw Poppy urge the other woman closer to Mischa, turning to call the rest of the models. Moments later the cameras were snapping group shots of a dozen dazzling models with Mischa at their centre and Poppy far away on the edge of the group.

From deep inside Orsino's churning gut a tiny sliver of warmth rose and spread.

His mouth tipped in a sharp smile of satisfaction as Mischa turned his head to the red-headed siren at the end of the group but failed to catch her eye.

A ripple of relief and pleasure filled Orsino as the group broke up and Poppy turned away so swiftly her long skirt flared behind her.

She looked up. Her eyes caught his and Orsino's heart thudded at what he thought he read there.

Orsino strode towards her like a man on a mission and Poppy's heart leapt. The strain of keeping a smile on her face this past hour through the preparty photos had been almost too much to bear.

Seeing Mischa had brought it all home again. That dreadful night when, distraught and alone, she'd turned to him because Orsino hadn't been there.

The things Mischa had whispered in her ear, about always desiring her, wanting a future with her, about how her husband had never been right for her.

The awful shame she felt when she'd emerged later from the shower after trying to scrub Mischa's touch from her skin, to find the man she loved staring at her as if she'd crawled out from under a rock.

Worst of all, the way Orsino had turned on his heel when she'd started to explain. He'd left her bereft and ashamed.

Now he covered the space between them, his long, powerful legs eating up the distance. His face told her nothing and the hairs on her nape prickled. He must have seen her with Mischa.

Poppy braced for a sarcastic remark. Or even for him to stalk past and punch the other man's lights out.

Instead he stopped before her—big, bold and potently handsome. Dimly she was aware of heads turning. His nostrils flared as if dragging in air, his gaze pinioned her so that moving away was beyond her.

Then slowly he reached for her, took her cold hand in his warm one, closing long fingers over it. Her heart crashed against her breastbone as he lifted her hand to his lips, slowly savouring the taste of her.

Poppy's nipples budded and the steel bands of tension around her ribs shattered and fell.

She sighed and swayed closer, unable to resist.

Orsino wrapped his arm around her waist and hauled her to him. His other hand went to her hair, inexorably pulling her head back. His mouth descended on hers in a flagrant display of alpha male power and sexual potency Poppy hadn't a hope of resisting.

A voice inside whispered he was putting on the macho display for Mischa's benefit.

Then his mouth moved on hers and there was no more thinking. Poppy's mind shut down as she sank into him. All thought, all doubts, were eclipsed as she finally gave up fighting her feelings. She stopped pretending.

Here in Orsino's arms was the one place in the world she wanted to be.

Nothing else mattered, not even pride.

It was an evening of elegance and glamour. The beautiful old chateau came to life under the light of massed candles, roaring fires and camera flashes. A buffet banquet fit for royalty was served and there was dancing in the ballroom where they'd filmed in period costume. Lights swayed on the dark river and flambeaux lit the exquisite gardens.

Through it all Poppy only had eyes for Orsino, basking in the warmth of him at her side, his smile, the touch of his arm at her back.

It was as if the intervening years hadn't happened.

No, more than that.

Poppy felt closer to him, more attuned than she'd been in their short-lived marriage. That had been tempestuous, passionate and exciting. What she felt now was no less passionate, but more mature. They were the feelings of a woman for her mate, her love, rather than those of an immature girl, swept up in the throes of her first love affair.

She'd tried so long to deny her feelings for Orsino.

Instead she'd fallen for him all over again. Not just for the dashing, charismatic darling of the jet set, but for the thoughtful, caring man who worked behind the scenes to make life better for people he didn't know. For the man who'd taken on an aggressive, chauvinist bully without a thought for his own disabled state. For the man who'd shown her tenderness and caring instead of cynicism and hatred.

Was that forgiveness?

Finally Orsino had let her see beyond his facade of casual indifference and privilege, revealing the intensely private man she'd never really understood. Now she guessed a little of how he'd been shaped by his lonely childhood, devoid of parental love.

Her betrayal must have devastated a man who'd never been able to rely on love.

A heated coil of guilt twisted within.

Had he thought she'd lied about her love for him?

Of course he had.

Now she even had some idea of how much his trips into the wild meant. Maybe he hadn't been rejecting her after all. She realised now they were an essential part of Orsino. Despite his easy charm, the glamorous social scene wasn't his natural milieu. If she wasn't mistaken, he was a man who drew strength from solitude and physical challenge. Despite his large family he'd been essentially alone most of his life.

Poppy breathed deep, trying to harness the raw emotions filling her. Fear. Excitement. A bud of hope.

These weeks had revealed how very much Orsino meant to her.

She couldn't put off the inevitable. The shoot was over. Tonight was the final celebration and media launch. Tomorrow everyone went their separate ways. Yet she hadn't discussed the future with Orsino. She'd been too scared he planned simply to leave.

How could she have been such a coward?

She'd pushed him away once when she'd needed him, when her mother died. Hadn't she learned from that?

They'd both made mistakes. Neither, she guessed, had been ready for marriage. Now she was tired of running, tired of pretending.

Poppy's heart drummed loud in her ears as she looked up at his proud profile, the curl of ink-dark hair on his brow, the strong nose and solid jaw.

Would he listen this time?

Had anything changed for him?

Her heart dived as trepidation filled her. She had to find

out. She'd been a coward years ago, hurting them both in the process. It was time to be brave.

'If you'll excuse us?' Poppy linked her arm through Orsino's and drew him away from a cluster of Baudin executives. 'We just need to...' Poppy used her trademark smile as she gestured to the far side of the room, as if she'd noticed someone they needed to see.

'Where are we going?' Orsino's deep voice skimmed her flesh, making her shiver.

'Somewhere private.' Poppy sensed his gaze sharpen.

Thankfully he didn't question, just let her lead him past knots of models and executives, socialites and minor royals, till at last the noise receded.

They stopped in a secluded hexagonal room jutting out over the river. It held a writing desk and chair and a wide window seat that ran beneath the angled walls.

There were no lights bar the flood of moonlight and the torches outside. This would be easier in the dark. Poppy closed the door behind her with a quiet snick.

Immediately Orsino reached for her, his hand covering her breast, the other wrapping round her waist as his head dipped.

'I do like a woman who shows initiative,' he purred in a bass rumble against her throat as he gathered her to him. Instantly her body melted, lax in his hold, liquid heat firing at her core. Her breathing was choppy, needy, like the way she clung to him.

One touch was all it took.

But through the fierce surge of sexual excitement rose the knowledge that what she needed from Orsino was more even than this.

A sob rose in her throat as fear stifled joy. When he knew what she had to tell him would it be the end?

She wasn't sure how she'd survive if he left her again. But she couldn't go on, living from hour to hour, waiting for him to declare it was over. She had to try.

'Poppy?' His hot breath hazed her cheek as he straight-ened. 'What is it?'

For an instant she clung tight to his shoulders, wish-ing they could stay just like this. Then she straightened, pushed him back.

'We need to talk.'

'Talk?' He sounded confused, as if she spoke a foreign language. She didn't blame him. Her body was on fire. The urge to lose herself in his embrace and the ecstasy she knew he could give her was strong.

But that wouldn't last.

Poppy took a half pace back and stiffened her shoulders.

'I have something important you need to hear. Will you listen?'

With the moonlight behind him she couldn't read his ex-pression, just the lift of his straight shoulders.

'Yes.'

He didn't sound encouraging. 'I want you to promise.'

'What?' His tone was sharp.

'Promise you'll hear me out. You won't leave till I've finished.'

Silence reigned. Did he, too, remember that night five years ago when he'd walked away, refusing to let her fin-ish what she had to say? Distraught as she'd been, anger had buoyed her through the intervening months when she'd faced the fallout of his desertion. Now the anger had died.

Poppy clasped her hands, tension winding through her.

'If it means so much to you.'

'It does.'

'Very well.' He inclined his head and she breathed a sigh of relief. 'I'll stay.'

'Do you want to sit?' She waved to the chair.

'I'm fine.' He paused, waiting. 'What is it, Poppy?' Did she imagine warmth in his tone?

'I want to tell you about the past.'

'Not my favourite topic. Haven't we said it all?'

She shook her head, the movement jerky as tendons and muscles stiffened. 'No. Not everything.'

Poppy heaved a deep breath then realised she had no idea where to start. How could she make him understand?

Orsino moved, his hand brushing hers, and she jumped. Swallowing, she turned away and walked to the window, barely registering the exquisite scene of river and formal garden washed in silvery light. It would be easier if she didn't look at him.

'When I met you I wasn't looking for a lover, much less a husband.' The words tumbled into waiting silence. Poppy pressed her hands together. 'I was focused on my job. On making a success of myself.'

'I remember.' There was a sour note in Orsino's voice. He'd accepted her work but never gone out of his way to support it.

Poppy swung round, needing him to understand. 'You heard what my father was like. Can you blame me for wanting to escape? For wanting to build a life for myself and my mother, free of him?'

'Of course not.' Orsino's bulk loomed larger in the dim light.

'I know you work hard, Orsino. I've seen the programs you're involved in.' Those glimpses into his philanthropic interests had amazed her. 'But you never had to build yourself up from nothing. You had family money behind you.'

'Actually, I live off my investments. I'm not reliant on the family trust.'

Poppy shook her head. 'But it was *there* if you needed it—a safety net. I started with no money, just luck and sheer hard work to support me. You said the other day I'd chased media attention.' She stuck her chin up. 'Maybe I did. Where's the harm in that when no one was hurt and it did my career a lot of good?'

She forced herself back to the point. 'I'm trying to explain why my career is so important.'

'So you'd never have to rely on your father.'

Poppy nodded. 'More than that. So I'd never have to rely on *anyone*, *ever*, apart from myself.'

She rubbed her hands up her arms, half turning to the river. 'Growing up watching my parents made me determined not just to escape but never to be weak the way my mother was. Never to allow myself to rely on anyone, make excuses for them, hang on to them even when it was a mistake. I wanted... I've *always* wanted to be independent.'

Poppy drew a deep breath. 'It wasn't just financial independence I dreamed of. It was complete self-reliance. That way—' she paused, her throat closing '—I'd never be hurt. You see?' She spun round to face him.

In the gloom he shook his head.

Poppy clamped her hands on her elbows. She'd never shared this with anyone. Could she make him understand?

'I didn't want love. I didn't trust it. Love was something that made a woman weak—made her a walkover for any man who wanted to grind her underfoot.'

'I never did that to you!'

He moved towards her and she put out a hand to stop him. 'Hear me out.'

'I'm not like your father, Poppy. Don't pretend I am.' His voice had lost the clipped anger she remembered from past arguments. It sounded raw, pained.

'I'm not saying you were. Not physically abusive anyway.'

'Now that's—'

'Please!' She put up one hand and he juddered to a halt mere feet away. 'What I'm trying to say is that it wasn't about *you*, at least not in the way you thought. It was about *me*.' Now it came to revealing her innermost demons Poppy's larynx froze, the words emerging as a hoarse whisper. 'I thought falling in love meant disaster. That it meant laying myself open to the worst kind of hurt and betrayal. So when I fell for you...' She couldn't help it—her head drooped, cutting the connection that sizzled between them even in the dark.

'When I fell in love with you it was paradise and hell together. I'd never felt so ecstatic, or so fearful.'

'I'd never have hurt you, Poppy. Surely you know that. I'd never raise my hand to a woman.'

'I know.' She looked up and caught the gleam of his penetrating gaze on her. 'I know you'd never hurt me physically. But there are other ways.'

She swung away to the far window, her hand going to the rich velvet curtain drawn open at the casement.

'I loved you despite my fear, despite all caution. I loved you so much.' She swallowed and made herself go on. 'But it wasn't an equal partnership. You never said you loved me, just that you needed me.' Poppy blinked and the flaming torches in the grounds shed crystalline shards of light as she forced back hot tears.

'It seemed I was the one being made to change to fit your life, because you didn't approve of my long hours, or the times a shoot would take me from you. You didn't approve of Mischa, either, but he was my friend and mentor, the man who'd helped me since I was fifteen.'

Behind her Orsino remained silent.

'You didn't change your life for me. You shut me away from the only thing important to you—your treks. Then I realised I was making excuses for you, like my mother used to for my father. Telling myself it didn't matter that you left me behind without a second glance, though you always wanted me on tap when you were back in London. Telling myself it didn't matter that you wouldn't make an effort to accommodate *my* needs and *my* career.'

Poppy's breath shuddered from tight lungs. 'Even then, when I saw myself becoming like her, I didn't want to give you up.' She swung round and faced the big, taut man standing like a graven statue in the moonlight.

'Do you have any idea how terrifying it was to love you,

understanding you didn't care for me the way I did you? Knowing I was turning into the sort of woman I'd vowed never to become?'

'Poppy.' Orsino stepped close then stopped, his arm falling as she kept talking. If she didn't get this out now she'd never have the guts to tell the truth.

'I closed in on myself when my mother died. You tried to comfort me but all I could think of was how she'd turned herself inside out explaining away her husband's behaviour. I saw myself doing the same and knew I needed to distance myself, keep some emotional independence if I was going to survive.'

'That's why you told me to fly to Kathmandu for the climb I'd planned?'

Poppy shrugged. 'You wanted to. You didn't take much persuading. When I mentioned it you were off like a shot.' Her gaze snagged on his face. 'You didn't love me.'

'Is that what you told yourself when you went to bed with your precious Mischa?' An undercurrent of anger turned Orsino's words into a deep rumble, as if tectonic plates shifted beneath the earth's surface.

'It's no excuse. Like grief and red wine on an empty stomach were no excuse. But yes, I thought it.' Poppy wrapped her arms tight around herself as she blinked back tears she refused to let fall.

'I was worn out and desperate. I loved you so much it terrified me. I'd just buried the only other person I loved. I told myself I had to learn from her mistakes.'

'You say I was one of them?' His tone was grim.

'Weren't you?' Her head reared up. 'If you'd really loved me would you have been so eager to race away with your mates to climb a mountain on the other side of the world? Mischa was the one left to pick up the pieces.'

Poppy shook her head, her brief flare of anger dying. 'I was a fool. I was miserable and furious and drunk. I let him hold me and comfort me and—'

'You've said enough!' Orsino spoke through gritted teeth. Even in the gloom she saw the tense line of his clenched jaw.

'No, Orsino, I haven't. You wouldn't let me explain then. You just turned on your heel and left me there, alone.' She gulped. 'I tried for months to reach you. Letters returned, calls unanswered, emails unopened. You did a brilliant job of cutting me out of your life.' Pain throbbed through her. 'I tried again the other day but you made it clear you didn't want to know.' Poppy breathed deep and told herself the only way was forward. She refused to play by Orsino's rules any more.

'What you refused to hear was that, though Mischa and I kissed—' she couldn't believe she blushed '—though we ended up on the bed together, we did *not* have sex.'

Her words died into complete silence. Nothing moved, not even Orsino.

'When he touched me I realised it wasn't Mischa I wanted.' The tears she'd held back so long leaked silently down her cheeks. 'It was *you*. I wanted you to hold me. I needed your arms around me. Your voice saying you'd take care of me and it would be all right.'

Still Orsino stood as if turned to stone.

'That was when I realised how badly I was using him, my only real friend, because I couldn't have you. Because the man I loved didn't care enough to stay with me. And because I'd pushed you away.'

Poppy lifted a palm and swiped the wetness off her cheek. 'When you found me in the shower I'd stripped off my clothes and was trying to wash his touch off. I felt so… unclean, so guilty that I'd let what started as genuine sympathy get out of hand.'

'But you admitted you'd been with him!'

Poppy wiped her other cheek with a trembling hand.

'You'd already stalked in, ranting about seeing Mischa leave half undressed. I told you we'd kissed in the bedroom and that I regretted what I'd done. Before I could say any more you turned without a single word and walked out of my life.'

The memory spurted fury into her blood. How could he have left without hearing her out?

She jammed her hands on her hips, waiting.

'Why tell me this now?'

Poppy's head jerked back at the harsh crack of his voice. But she refused to be cowed or silenced again.

'Because it still matters to me. I told myself it didn't— that you, we, were in the past.' She drew herself up and met his regard unflinching, despite the churning fear in her belly. 'I was wrong. It does matter because I never stopped loving you.' Her words were defiant. 'That's why I had to tell you the whole truth.'

Because she'd hoped there was a chance to build something better from the ashes of their past.

Poppy thought Orsino's silence would break her. It went on so long every nerve stretched taut.

But it wasn't the silence that destroyed her.

It was his words.

'No! You're lying. It's not possible. It can't be.'

CHAPTER THIRTEEN

ORSINO LUMBERED THROUGH the antechambers like a man punch-drunk. More than once the floor tilted and rose up to meet him and he had to grab at a wall or doorframe to steady himself. The sound of music and voices came in waves, swelling to a roar in his ears then dying to nothing as Poppy's words hammered into his brain.

We did not have sex.

Because I never stopped loving you.

She was doing his head in. Playing with him.

Was this her revenge for the way he'd left her high and dry years before?

Was Poppy really so calculating and cruel?

He'd believed many things but never that.

Where the hell was she? He had to find her.

Orsino had no idea how long it had been since she'd turned and left him. Time had waned and stretched. Was it minutes or hours? Surely it couldn't be so long.

He searched for the dark flame of her long hair, the sinuous body in full-length purple, the glitter of gems and the proud thrust of her chin.

She'd looked like a queen, exquisitely regal and untouchable. Even with tears silvering her cheeks in the moonlight she'd had a power about her, a force that held him in check, awed not just by her words, but by *her*, the woman who turned him inside out and wrung him dry.

He'd felt empty inside, watching her battle her emotions. As if someone had reached in and ripped out his vital organs.

He swallowed convulsively, groping for the panelled wall, bile rising. What she'd said! How could she expect him to believe it? If what she said was true that meant that for five long years...

Orsino sagged against the wood panelling.

No. He refused to go there. He couldn't.

He squinted, surveying the throng in the next room through the open double doors. Colour and glitter and acres of bare flesh. But no Poppy.

He sank back, his whole body shuddering. He had to find her. He had to—

'Well, well. If it's not the celebrated hero. I have to say you look like you should be in a hospital bed, not propping up a wall. Or have you just had too much champagne?'

'Mischa.' Orsino grimaced on the name as he stumbled upright and slitted his eyes.

He couldn't even find the energy to dredge hatred for the man who surveyed him speculatively, pale eyebrows raised.

'I can't say it's a pleasure to see you again,' the other man said, his lip curling.

'I don't give a damn whether you're pleased.' Orsino shook his head, trying to clear it. 'Where is she?'

Mischa took his time raising a crystal tumbler to his mouth. With his too-perfect tailoring and languid movements, he looked so cool that Orsino battled the urge to force the information he needed.

'You've lost someone? How careless of you.' Mischa's light eyes glittered with something like hatred.

Orsino's fists bulged. Adrenaline pumped hard through his arteries as his body readied for action. But he held back.

'Don't play games. Where's Poppy?'

'Give me one good reason why I should tell you.'

'Because—' Orsino leaned into the other man's space '—she's my wife.'

To do him credit Mischa didn't flinch. Maybe he'd underrated the man.

'The wife you abandoned and ignored for the past five years?'

If Mischa thought anything he could say had the power to hurt Orsino now, he was badly mistaken. It wasn't possible to inflict more pain.

'That would be the one.' Orsino spoke through gritted teeth as he leaned closer. 'Where is she?'

Mischa faltered back a half step, this time reading something feral in Orsino's eyes.

'She's gone.'

'Gone?'

'Left.' Mischa paused. 'Alone.'

Orsino's knees buckled and he lurched back against the wall.

'She couldn't have gone.' His voice was a scratch of protest.

'You mean she couldn't have walked out on you?' Pale eyes skewered him. 'Why not? She obviously learned the tactic from an expert.' He paused as if wanting to see Orsino squirm then shrugged and turned away.

'Wait!' Orsino straightened, his arm outstretched. 'Is it true?'

Once he'd been too proud to speak to this guy. Now his pride was dust. He had to know.

'Is what true?'

'Poppy said you and she… That you'd never…'

Mischa swung around, his Slavic cheekbones prominent in a face drawn tight with emotion. 'What? That we'd never had sex? Is that what you're trying to spit out?' He bared his teeth. 'After all this time you're asking?'

Orsino nodded. 'Yes.' It was a harsh rasp of sound, ripped from the depths of his tortured soul.

Mischa took his time replying. 'Why ask me? The answer's obvious. You already know what happened that night.'

He spun round and strode across the room, closing the doors behind him, leaving Orsino alone in the darkness.

CHAPTER FOURTEEN

AFTER SCANNING THE hotel lobby, Poppy settled in her seat, flipping open a magazine. Her gaze met familiar violet eyes and she tilted her head, critically examining the photo of herself, half reclining on a rich brocade coverlet, her hair rippling around her. They'd been right to choose the ruby red for that dress. It complemented her pale skin and the fortune in gems she wore.

Poppy remembered the day mere weeks ago when that shot had been taken. No wonder her eyes held that slumberous come-hither look. Her mouth looked fuller, too. An hour before she'd been in Orsino's bed. She could still recall the taste of his demanding mouth on hers, the hot frenzy of need as he tormented her almost to breaking point before rewarding her ardour with a shuddering, soul-searing climax.

She'd felt well-loved. Physically, and she would have sworn, emotionally.

Poppy's mouth flattened.

That was before. She couldn't fool herself any longer that he cared.

Had it been worth it? Giving herself to him again?

Ecstasy while it lasted and pure hell now. Sometimes only the pain seemed real.

At least she understood why she hadn't been able to make a complete break before, why she'd gone running to Orsino the moment he crooked his finger.

Because she still loved him.

Maybe realising it was the first step in killing her feelings for him. Only a masochist would love a man who refused so blatantly to believe.

Poppy scrabbled at the glossy page, almost tearing it in her eagerness to turn it to something other than her own face, revealing how Orsino had made her feel.

Not any more. The utter bleakness of her life was a grey wall locking her in, even as she forced herself to go through the motions of living. Like now, waiting for her blind date.

If she could have avoided this she would, but auctioning off lunch with Poppy Graham at a swanky hotel had been a major fundraiser for the women's shelter. She couldn't back out now, especially since Mr Rossi had paid such a huge sum for the privilege.

A shiver rippled down her spine. So long as he realised it was just lunch he was getting for his money.

Across the foyer firm footsteps sounded and for a moment Poppy thought she recognised that decisive tread. The hairs rose on her arms and nape, but she kept her head down, gazing unseeing at the page before her.

Where was Orsino now? Visiting one of his charities in some far-flung corner of the globe? On a new trek?

'Poppy.'

Her head jerked up as if pulled by a string. Sweet piercing pain shot through her chest as she met familiar dark eyes. Every muscle and sinew in her body froze.

He looked different, she realised with shock. Orsino's proud, decisive features appeared gaunt, hollows grooved deep in his cheeks, his eyes sunken.

Yet he looked wonderful. Her stupid heart battered her ribs as if trying to escape so it could flop like a landed fish at his feet.

'Orsino!' It was a hiss of dismay. Of all the hotels in London why did he have to choose this one? What a cruel irony of fate. 'What are you doing here?'

'Looking for you.'

For her? She shook her head, unable to believe her ears.

'I'm meeting someone.' The words blurted out, a rebuff. She cast an anxious gaze towards the grand entry. Where was the man? She'd rather face a hundred blind dates than sit here trading chitchat with her husband.

'Yes, me.' Orsino's voice hadn't changed. It was as full of self-assurance as ever.

'No. I'm meeting a Mr—'

'Rossi.' He nodded. 'I know.'

Poppy's stomach sank and her flesh grew tight. 'How do you know?'

An expression flitted across Orsino's dark features, too fast to be read. Yet she sensed a change in him. No longer proud and authoritative but...could it be...hesitant?

She looked at his wide-legged stance, his fists anchored deep in his trouser pockets, and felt an unfamiliar vibe emanate from him. Slowly she closed the magazine and stood. In her heels she was just half a head shorter than him.

'Rossi was my mother's maiden name.'

Poppy blinked as his meaning sank slowly into her numbed brain. Horror stirred in her belly. He couldn't mean—

'*You* bid on me at the charity auction?'

He shrugged. Never had the casual Mediterranean gesture looked so stiff and cramped.

'I thought you wouldn't meet me if I rang.'

'You got that right.' What did he think he was doing, meeting her under false pretences?

She spun around on her heel. 'I've got to go.'

His arm shot out as if to grab her then dropped to his side. 'Please.'

The one word drilled through her panic. She stilled, though her pulse raced like an out of control train.

'It's taken me days to track you down. You left without a trace. No one seemed to know where you'd gone.'

'Why do you want to see me?'

He rubbed a hand through his hair, tumbling glossy locks into disarray. 'I need to talk with you.'

Poppy shuddered. 'I can't.' She couldn't put herself through that particular brand of torture again.

'Please, Poppy.' His voice was urgent. It held a note she'd never heard before, one that turned her churning belly inside out. How much more could she bear? 'I heard you out. Won't you hear me?'

Across the room Poppy saw heads craning to watch.

'Not here.' The words spilled from her lips before she could snatch them back.

'No.' His hand curved around her elbow and shimmering heat suffused her. She wanted to yank out of his hold but her brain sent the wrong signals to her body. 'I've got a car outside.'

'I'm not going anywhere with you.'

His grim smile told her he'd anticipated that. 'Do you want to hear what I have to say with waiters listening in? Or here in the lobby?' He glanced at the onlookers. 'I suppose I could book us a room—'

'You've made your point, Orsino.' She grabbed her purse. 'Let's go.'

'This is your apartment?' The sense of space and light, as well as the magnificent photo of dawn breaking over a desert somewhere, made it instantly recognisable.

'It is.'

She swung around but there was nothing to read in Orsino's face apart from tension around the lips. A tension echoed in her own body.

Why was she doing this? Why had she let him bring her here instead of demanding answers in the car? Because sharing the intimacy of his sports car, cut off from the grey world sliding by around them, had been too much like sharing the intimacy of his bed. She'd felt again that tantalising sense that nothing mattered except the pair of them.

Abruptly Poppy turned. She strode to the door leading to the roof terrace. She couldn't bear to be closed in with him even in this airy room.

Orsino was there first, opening the door and ushering her out, turning on outdoor heaters to dispel the winter chill.

But nothing could counter the cold creeping into Poppy's veins. She turned her back on the stunning city view and leaned against the railing, facing him.

'I'm waiting.'

He stood before her, his big hands clenching and releasing, a muscle jerking in his jaw.

'Orsino?' Poppy frowned. Why didn't he spit it out? He'd never been anything less than articulate, even in his fury. Especially in his fury.

One tanned hand ploughed through his hair. He stood so close she saw the new scars on it, even imagined it shook.

Sudden panic gripped her. Surely there wasn't some complication from his injuries? Could that explain why he looked so haggard?

She took a half step towards him then stopped as he spoke. She wouldn't have recognised Orsino's voice, wouldn't have believed it to be his, except she saw his lips move.

'You said I never loved you. I didn't care enough to stay.' His eyes bored into her. 'You're right that I never said it, never—' His voice cracked and he scrubbed a hand over his jaw.

Poppy's heart contracted. So, he wasn't going to deny it. She felt the last tiny bud of hope wither.

'Nothing had prepared me for you, for the way I'd feel about you.' His lips curved in a travesty of a smile that wrenched at something deep inside. 'Women were always easy for me, you see. I never had to try hard.' He shook his head. 'But with you, right from the first it was different.'

Poppy realised her breathing had stopped and had to drag in air. 'How?'

'How? I couldn't take you for granted. I didn't want to. I…needed you, right from the beginning. You were…important to me.' Orsino's laugh was harsh. 'I'm not explaining this well.'

'Just tell me.' She felt stretched too tight, yearning for the impossible, forcing herself to stay where she was, hands braced behind her on the railing.

'I couldn't *not* have you. I'm not just talking about in my bed, but in my life.' He paused to drag in a stertorous breath. 'I'd have done anything to keep you, even marry you.'

'You make it sound like a death sentence.' That was her prerogative, surely. She was the one who distrusted marriage.

His eyebrows rose. 'You think I wanted a wife? After witnessing my parents' relationship erode into nothing?' He shook his head. 'You weren't the only one set on independence. For me the ultimate pleasure has always been just me against the wilderness.' Orsino's eyes blazed. 'I've always been a loner. Relationships were short term and shallow, based on sex and lots of it.

'And then I met you.'

His words were harsh. Did he blame her for making him want her? For disrupting his life?

She wanted to wail: what about her? But Poppy kept her mouth closed. She'd already bared her soul.

The flow of words ended. He walked beyond her and grabbed the railing, hands splayed wide, broad shoulders open. He should have looked like the lord of all he surveyed, except his hands were bleached white by his tight grip and even in profile his grimace was obvious.

That's how she made him feel. Why did he haul her here just to tell her how unhappy she'd made him?

Poppy turned towards the door.

His arm shot out, hard fingers circling her wrist. Instantly heat flared and spread under her skin. A familiar heat. A longing.

No! This couldn't be.

He must have realised the same thing for his hand dropped as if he'd touched a live circuit.

'I can't do this, Orsino.' He was tearing her apart.

'Wait, Poppy. Give me a few more minutes.'

'Why?' Bracing herself for pain she raised her eyes. His gaze glittered with a febrile heat.

'Because I need to apologise.'

Apologise?

Suddenly Poppy was sinking onto a padded seat, her legs as wobbly as fresh-cooked spaghetti.

'Don't look so shocked.' His voice wasn't quite steady. 'I know I deserve it but—' He palmed the back of his neck, staring down at her as if he could see into the darkest corners of her soul.

Panic rose. After all he'd done, *and all he'd not done*, it was probably too late for them.

'Marrying was a huge mistake. I see that now.'

He watched her face turn parchment white and cursed himself for inflicting more pain.

'Because I hurt you. Because—' the words tasted bitter on his tongue '—I hadn't the first clue how to be a decent husband. All I knew was that I needed you. The more I had you, the more I needed you.'

Poppy had opened up a whole new world of wanting to him and it had terrified him.

'I was selfish. I couldn't understand why I wasn't enough for you. Why you had to spend your time working when I had enough money to support us both.'

Poppy frowned. 'But it was my career.'

Orsino nodded, wincing at the self-absorbed fool he'd been. 'I know. I gave lip service to it but never really understood.' He swiped his hand over his jaw, wishing the right words would come. 'Not till you told me about your parents and what your career meant. I'd thought you were playing at modelling.'

'Playing?' Her voice rose. Fire blazed in her eyes. He felt better seeing her like this, ready to fight from her corner. Watching her slump into the chair, her expression defeated, had gutted him.

'I told you I was self-absorbed. I could say I was used to mixing with women whose jobs were fill-ins until they landed a rich husband but that's no excuse. When I saw you were serious I began to get jealous.'

She stiffened. 'Of Mischa.'

Orsino spread his arms. 'You shared a relationship that excluded me. You turned to him so often. I couldn't understand why I wasn't enough for you. You're right. I'd led a life of privilege too long. It took the shock of our split, and burying myself in work, discovering I could do something useful for other people, for me to mature. Seeing the burdens other people face daily without complaint put my woes into perspective. Back then I was jealous of your work because it took you away. Those 4:00 a.m. starts when I wanted to drag you back to bed—'

'You thought I wanted to leave you then?' She looked dazed.

He shrugged. 'I was insecure. I thought you were finding excuses.'

'Excuses not to be with you?' She shook her head. 'I was head over ears in love with you. I *told* you.'

Heat washed up his throat and over his cheeks, making even his ears burn. He couldn't remember blushing before. But then he'd never felt so ashamed.

'You didn't believe me?' Poppy's eyes widened till they seemed to consume her face.

'I thought it was just—' He gestured vaguely. 'I thought it was passion, not love.' Before she could respond he continued. 'I was wrong. I know now I hurt you. It's just that no one had ever loved me before.' Orsino heard how pathetic that sounded and hurried on. He wasn't after sympathy. 'Not even my parents. The exception is Lucca, but that's different.' That was something they were born with.

'I was so happy with you, Poppy. But all the time at the back of my mind—no, not my mind—somewhere else, some part of me that worked on instinct—I was half waiting for it to end.'

'Oh, Orsino.'

The look on her face carved another chunk out of his heart. How he'd hurt her.

'I'm sorry, Poppy. You have no idea how sorry I am. I should have supported your career, not complained about it. I should have been there for you more.'

He swallowed, recalling that last, terrible week.

'When your mother died I tried to comfort you, to be a good husband. I couldn't bear to see you hurting like that, but I couldn't help. Nothing I did was right.'

'Because I pushed you away. I was terrified of leaning on you, Orsino.' Her eyes held his. 'It wasn't you, it was me.'

He shook his head, knowing this was his fault. 'It shouldn't have made a difference. I should have realised you weren't yourself. But when you pushed me away it all rose to the surface—the way my mother shunned Lucca and me, as if even looking at us hurt, the way my father ignored us all as much as he could.' His lips thinned. He'd let childhood fears take over when he should have stood firm and been the man she needed him to be.

'I felt rejected and it was as if the blow I'd been waiting for had finally fallen. That you didn't need me after all.'

Poppy shook her head, her mouth working, and he wanted to reach for her hand. He forced himself not to move.

'I got to the airport and the flight was called and suddenly I knew I couldn't go.' His lips pulled tight in a mirthless smile. 'I'd like to say it was because you needed me and in part it was, but above it was my own overriding need to be with you. So I turned round and came back to the apartment.'

'Where you saw Mischa leaving.' Poppy's voice was flat.

Orsino nodded. 'I came in expecting the worst, wanting desperately to hear I was wrong, but not really listening. And when I thought you'd betrayed me it was one more rejection.'

He blinked, his eyes burning as his vision blurred. 'With you I'd known real happiness. I'd begun to hope maybe they weren't just words when you said "I love you".'

He swallowed over jagged glass. 'I should have stayed to hear you out. Hell! I should have been there comforting you from the first, not leaving it to Mischa. But I was convinced I knew what was coming and I couldn't bear to hear it. That's why I ran away. That's why I made sure you couldn't reach me for months afterwards. Because I was a coward.'

Warm fingers closed around his and shock thundered through him.

'You weren't the only one, Orsino. I should have told you about my parents. About my hang-ups.' Dark velvet eyes drew him close. 'I shouldn't have turned away from you.'

'Why should you have wanted me there? I couldn't even tell you I loved you.'

Poppy's face drew tight, pain scoring deep.

Orsino couldn't bear it. He dropped to his knees before her as she sat. Her fingers were icy as he massaged them.

'I couldn't tell you because I was frightened.'

Once more her eyes rounded. 'You're not frightened of anything. You're fearless.'

He laughed, the sound harsh on his lips. 'You have no idea.' Even now his belly was twisting like a python shimmying up a tree. 'I can face cliff faces and deserts and tundra, but telling my wife how I really feel scared me witless. It still does.'

'How do you feel, Orsino?' She sounded as breathless as he felt.

He swallowed hard.

'I've loved you since the moment I saw you. At the beginning I thought it was lust but it's far more. You make me whole. When I realised it was love I was petrified of telling you, fearing it would make me weak. That's why I never said the words. I was living my life with a chunk of myself missing until I found you. And then when I left you—'
Yawning blackness filled his vision.

'You loved me then?' Kneeling before Poppy, holding her hands, he felt her tremble. Her eyes shimmered and his chest seemed to cave in on itself.

'I've always loved you. That's why in five years I've never been with another woman.'

She stared, astonished. He had no pride left, not with Poppy. Pride and doubt and fear had stood between them too long.

'Why do you think my schedule has been so hectic? How do you think I've fitted in so many extreme sports and treks as well as my work as a charity administrator? I had to work off my frustration somehow. I've had to channel all my energies into things other than sex and loving you.'

'But those women. I saw photos of you everywhere.'

'Companions at galas and dinners. I didn't take one to bed. How could I, when the only woman I wanted was you?'

Poppy's mouth sagged open but no sound came out.

'When we met again I was desperate for you. I almost exploded the first time you touched me. Why do you think we had sex against a wall and didn't make it to a bed? For five years I'd been dreaming of you, wanting you.' He stretched out his other hand and dared to feather a touch along her cheekbone. She felt like satin and warmth and home. Orsino's belly cramped.

'There's no one but you for me, Poppy.'

Her eyes squeezed shut and he felt her shiver.

'What changed your mind? Did you talk to Mischa when I left? Did he tell you we hadn't slept together? You made it clear you didn't believe me.'

Her words were terse. She thought he came to her now because Mischa had persuaded him of her innocence. That he didn't have faith in her word alone. Who could blame her?

Orsino surged to his feet, nausea rising. It was his own fault. What reason did she have to trust him?

He turned away and braced himself on the railing. His head sagged and his breath came in ragged gasps.

He'd lost her. She'd gone beyond forgiveness.

'Mischa didn't tell me. The man hates my guts. You know he loves you?' How could she not know? It was glaringly obvious.

'He refused to tell me anything, especially where you were. When I asked him what had happened five years ago he told me I already knew.'

Poppy's hissed intake of air was loud in the silence.

'Either I believed what you told me or I didn't. That's when I knew. The answer had been there all the time if I stopped to think about *you*, the woman you really are.'

Orsino's hands shook as he clenched the railing.

'I've been wrong about you. I accused you out of fear.'

'But you didn't believe me when I told you in the chateau! You said it wasn't possible.'

He shook his head. 'I didn't want to believe it because it meant I'd sentenced us to years of hell for nothing. How could I live with that? How could I have done that to the woman I loved?' His whole body quaked. 'You're better off without me.'

Even as he said it a voice inside howled in despair. How could he move on without Poppy? He didn't know how to let her go.

'So you pushed me away instead.' Pain threaded her voice and something died inside. She didn't sound like a woman reunited with the man she loved. She sounded like a woman who'd had her fill of hurt. Because of him.

Light fingers brushed his cheek, smearing wetness.

'Orsino!' Shock pared her features to taut lines. 'You're—'

'I haven't cried since I was seven. I thought I'd forgotten how.' His attempt at a laugh was pathetic.

Her eyes met his, deep violet and so beautiful he never wanted to look away. Till he saw the shadows of regret haunting them even now she knew the truth.

'Oh, Orsino.' Poppy leaned into him, her arms lifting as if to wrap around him, but he moved lightning fast, grabbing her wrists and holding her back.

'No! Don't feel sorry for me. I don't want that.' Selfishly he wanted so much more. 'I've made mistakes that have cost us both. I don't deserve your sympathy.' He'd hurt her so badly, not once but twice. How could she trust him after he'd failed her like that?

For a pulse beat and another and another, their eyes held. He knew she read his regret and his determination.

Finally Poppy tugged her arms free.

That one movement destroyed something inside. He felt bereft. But what sort of man would hang on to her by playing on her heartstrings?

'So now you know.' Orsino cleared his throat and stepped away. 'You deserved the truth before we go our separate ways.'

'That's what you want?' Her voice was a raw whisper, her eyes huge.

He watched for any sign she felt more than pity and regret for his stupidity. He saw nothing but shock.

She said nothing about being in love with him.

Hope died. He released the breath he'd held, waiting to hear those three words she'd once shared so willingly. He'd finally managed to kill her feelings when he'd rejected her confession at the chateau party.

'Are you ready to leave?' he asked abruptly, needing to end this. 'I'll drive you wherever you want to go.'

She stepped back and a leaden weight crushed his heart. 'No. I'll grab a taxi.'

CHAPTER FIFTEEN

ORSINO FOLLOWED THE receptionist's directions and stalked down the corridor to the conference room. His skin prickled just being in London's Chatsfield Hotel after all these years. It reminded him of his father's arrogant assumption that he'd drop everything to become the public face of the company.

He raked his hand across his chin, feeling the growth he hadn't bothered to shave. He wasn't in the mood for business, but Bettina had been insistent, if cagey, saying this was an opportunity not to be missed.

He should have been heading to the Cuillins this morning. What better way to test his recuperation than by tackling some of Scotland's most challenging climbs? He twitched his bad hand, wondering if he was kidding himself even attempting to climb again.

If he wasn't up to it physically then he'd have to find some other distraction. Something to dull the memory of Poppy saying goodbye. So far nothing had worked.

His stride faltered as pain swamped him.

Would he ever see her again except on billboards?

He didn't know which would be worse—seeing her and not being with her, or never laying eyes on her again.

The sooner he was away to Skye, the better. At least there he could be alone with his misery.

Orsino scowled. This Ms Beaufort had better have a worthwhile proposal or he'd be out of here like a shot.

He reached the door, knocked peremptorily and swung

into the conference room, only to pull up short as the ground fell away beneath his feet.

A tall woman rose from one of the swivel chairs at the table. With her back to the window the stream of daylight detailed her slim-fitting dark suit with its cinched-in waist. She had hair the colour of passion, pulled back high from her face.

'Poppy?' he croaked. He swiped his hand over bleary eyes. Was he seeing things?

She stepped around the table and he saw flawless legs and shapely feet in glossy black shoes so high she looked like some erotic fantasy come to life. Pearls circled her pale throat, drawing attention to the deep plunge of her charcoal suit, and the fact she wasn't wearing a shirt beneath it.

It *was* her.

Instinctively he inhaled as she approached, letting the delicate, fresh scent of her invade his senses.

His eyes dropped to glossy lips the colour of raspberries and he bit back a groan of longing.

'What are you…?' His words died as she stepped past him and snicked the door locked.

'Just making sure we're not disturbed,' she murmured as she walked back to the polished conference table.

'Poppy? What is this?' His head spun. It was all he could do not to grab her, bury his head in her neck and haul her up against him. 'Where's Ms Beaufort?'

Her hand strayed to her throat, as if she were nervous. Then she lifted her chin.

'You're looking at her.'

'I don't understand.' He'd had so little sleep lately. Could he be dreaming?

'I took a leaf out of your book and used my mother's maiden name.'

'Because?'

She folded her arms, bending one knee and jutting her hip out in a stance that was pure challenge. 'Because you made it painfully obvious last time that you were so racked with guilt you couldn't face being with me. Subterfuge seemed my only option.'

Poppy's heart dipped and she clenched her fingers into the sleeves of her jacket, pulling her folded arms in close.

Orsino's liquid dark eyes flared and his gaze dropped to the deep V of her cleavage as her breasts plumped higher. The heat in his eyes belied his stern expression and taut features.

A spark of hope flared. She wasn't too proud to use her natural assets to get what she wanted. The stakes were too high to chance failure. She leaned forward.

'I've got a business proposition for your charity work.' She swiped her tongue along her bottom lip, more nervous than she'd been on her first photo shoot, and was rewarded when Orsino's eyes flickered.

'You want to talk about *philanthropy*?' His head swung from side to side like a boxer who'd taken one too many hits and couldn't focus.

'Why not? You're not the only one with an interest.' She leaned back against the conference table, trying to project confidence.

Orsino's eyes narrowed. She'd known that sharp brain of his would click into gear quickly. She hurried on. 'My proposal will benefit your fundraising.'

'Really?'

'Absolutely.' She nodded to a nearby chair. 'Why don't you take a seat?'

'I'm fine standing.' He crossed his arms, reinforcing the lean strength of his broad chest beneath the jacket and plain shirt.

'You won't mind if I get comfortable.' She shimmied onto the table behind her, aware of Orsino's gaze zeroing like a laser onto her legs as her skirt rode up from just above the knee to reveal several inches of thigh.

Poppy took her time crossing her legs, hyperaware of the slide of silk stockings against her thighs. She suppressed a smile at the convulsive movement of Orsino's throat.

'You have a proposal?' His voice was rough but his eyes glittered as if he saw through her obvious tactic.

'How is your eyesight now? Still improving?'

'Almost normal.' He spread his hands. 'But time will tell.' He paused. 'You were saying?'

Poppy swallowed. What had seemed easy in theory was now impossibly daunting. The big man standing four square before her bore little resemblance to the emotionally wounded one who'd poured out his remorse and pushed her away when she'd tried to comfort him.

She grabbed her courage in both hands. She could do this. Failure wasn't an option.

'You do an excellent job raising money for your charities.'

'Thank you.'

'But they're a series of one-off events that catch the public attention for a short time.'

His eyebrows flattened. 'So?'

'What about a sustained approach? Awareness raising that goes on even when you're not risking your neck climbing a frozen waterfall or crossing a desert?'

'Go on.'

She had his attention. Perversely she felt a fillip of annoyance that he hadn't tried to gather her close and kiss her senseless.

Poppy recrossed her legs and satisfaction filled her as his gaze slid to the movement and lingered. Not so aloof after all. Deliberately she swung one foot, watching him follow the provocative movement of a shoe designed with one message: *Ravish Me*.

'I have contacts interested in contributing to a media campaign. They'd give their services for free.'

Orsino's gaze jerked up. 'Models?'

'Don't knock them,' she said before he could make a disparaging remark. 'People are drawn to beauty. It can sell a lot of ideas, not just luxury goods.'

'I wasn't being negative. We'll take all the help we can get.'

Poppy stared but read nothing in his expression. 'Not only models. Photographers and filmmakers.' She mentioned a couple of names that made Orsino's brows shoot up. 'We thought some advertisements and maybe a short documentary. Plus a series of fundraising events with some glamour thrown in.'

'It sounds too good to be true.' His stance, feet planted wide and arms crossed, told her he wasn't convinced.

'There are a couple of stipulations.'

'Are there indeed?' His deep voice grooved a hollow through her empty belly.

It was Poppy's turn to swallow as his gaze seared her. She lifted a hand to her necklace.

'You'd have to work with me, for one. I want to be part of it.'

'Why?'

Poppy shrugged. 'I'm not going to be a model all my life. I want to develop skills in other areas. This is a perfect opportunity while doing something worthwhile.'

He was silent so long nervous tension buzzed through her like swarming bees. She flushed, heat dousing her skin. Had she misjudged him? Had he pushed her away not for her sake but his?

'What else?' He stepped close, looming above her, and the room shrank.

She lifted her head, reminding herself she could do this.

'I don't just want to work with you.'

'No?' His hands dropped to his sides. Poppy watched them flex. 'What else do you want?'

Her hand went to her jacket. She slipped open a button

then another and the sides swung wide, revealing pale skin and a demi-cup bra of gossamer grey lace.

Orsino's chest rose mightily as he sucked in air. The planes of his face grew sharp, his nostrils pinching.

'You want sex?' He sounded strangled.

Poppy shrugged out of her jacket, feeling the cool air prickle her skin. Her nipples puckered. She'd never felt so exposed.

Why didn't he move?

'Yes,' she whispered, her throat clogging. She didn't know what to do with her hands, eventually planting them wide on the table. 'But I want more, too.'

'More?'

'I want to be your wife.' His eyes jerked up to snare on hers and she felt the beat of connection between them. 'I want us to live together, as husband and wife.'

'Is this some joke? Payback?'

Her heart plummeted. 'You think I'd play that sort of game?'

'No!' He swung his head from side to side as if trying to clear his head. 'But I can't believe...' He swallowed convulsively, the lines bracketing his mouth carving deep.

For long seconds Orsino stared. 'Is it possible?'

'Of course it's possible!' Her voice gathered strength. 'You were so busy beating yourself up about how you'd treated me you forgot about the fact that I love you.'

'You do? Still?' His eyes gleamed with a dark brilliance.

'I told you, remember? I don't need you to decide for me what I want or don't want.' It had hurt when he'd revealed his feelings only to push her away. Her chin jutted higher.

Slowly he smiled and Poppy's heart cracked, flooding her with warmth.

'I remember.' With one step he was so close she had to tilt her head back to meet his eyes. Her knees parted so he stood between them.

'I don't understand how you could still love me—' He

raised his hand when she would have spoken. 'I can't believe you forgive me for being so blind. But I'm grateful.' He brushed a stray lock of hair behind her ear. He was trembling as badly as she. 'I love you so much, Poppy.'

For one, long, glorious moment the world stood still as their gazes meshed. Poppy could swear she heard his heart beat with hers.

Then he cupped her breast and her eyes rolled back in pleasure and relief. It had been too long.

'Sex and marriage and working together. I can manage that.' Orsino dipped his head and nuzzled the sweet spot at the junction of her neck and shoulder. Poppy gasped as pleasure shot through her. She reached for him, was fumbling his belt undone, when he spoke again.

'Is that all?'

'No.' She dragged her eyes open and leaned away from his mouth. 'I want you to call your father.'

He stiffened, straightening to stare down at her.

'Just call him and find out why he wanted you to work for the family company.'

'Why?' There was no anger in Orsino's gaze, just curiosity.

'Because family is important.' Poppy thought of her mother and the bond they'd shared and her voice strengthened. 'I'm not saying he's perfect or even admirable. But there's a chance his offer was a sign he'd like to build bridges. Maybe he realised what he's missed out on all these years, being estranged.' Orsino deserved that chance that had been so long denied.

'One phone call,' he stipulated.

She nodded, her heart swelling that Orsino would consider this for her. 'Yes.'

Abruptly Orsino pushed her back till she lay across the polished table. Excitement rippled through her as he loomed over her and she read the dark intent in his eyes.

'Is that all?'

'One more thing.' She gasped as he bit her earlobe and liquid heat pooled in her belly.

'You drive a hard bargain, Mrs Chatsfield.'

Poppy's heart thudded. Mrs Chatsfield. She liked that.

His hand slid up beneath her skirt, stopping when it reached bare skin at the top of her stocking.

'Witch!'

Orsino's mouth plundered hers and the world spun. Happiness filled her. So much happiness she thought she might burst.

'What is it, this last thing?' He lifted his head and Poppy saw adoration in his eyes. She blinked hard.

'Poppy? My love, it's all right. I'll make it okay. What is it you want? Come on, it can't be that bad.'

'Not bad at all.' She cupped his beloved face in her hands. 'I want you to spend a little more time in England so we could start trying for a family.'

The slow grin that spread across his face was the most wonderful thing she'd ever seen.

'I love a woman who knows what she wants.' He flexed his hand against her breast and she bit down on a moan. 'You know, I've been thinking of pulling back a little on the more dangerous expeditions now there's so much administrative work. Making a family with you would be a whole new adventure.'

Her throat closed so the words wouldn't come. Instead she pulled him close and kissed him with all the love and happiness welling inside. Hope and forgiveness passed between them, binding them together.

Poppy slid her hands across his jaw, revelling in the strength and masculine roughness of his bristled chin.

Orsino's hand slipped higher beneath her skirt then stalled as it encountered nothing but bare skin and soft femininity. His head reared back and his eyes widened.

His voice was strangled. 'You're a dangerous woman,

Poppy. More dangerous than any mountain I could climb. You might just kill me yet.'

But there was satisfaction on his face as his hand explored. Poppy bucked beneath his touch as he unerringly found her most sensitive spot.

She grabbed his zipper. 'But I intend for us to live together for a long, long time.'

'Our very own happy-ever-after?' The look in his eyes would have melted the frozen arctic. 'I love you, Poppy, more than life itself. If that's what you want, I'll do my very best to deliver.'

Then he sealed the promise with a kiss that obliterated all the pain of the past and foreshadowed everything she wanted for the future.

* * * * *

If you enjoyed this book,
look out for the next instalment of
THE CHATSFIELD:
HEIRESS'S DEFIANCE
by Lynn Raye Harris,
coming next month.

Mills & Boon® Hardback
November 2014

ROMANCE

A Virgin for His Prize	Lucy Monroe
The Valquez Seduction	Melanie Milburne
Protecting the Desert Princess	Carol Marinelli
One Night with Morelli	Kim Lawrence
To Defy a Sheikh	Maisey Yates
The Russian's Acquisition	Dani Collins
The True King of Dahaar	Tara Pammi
Rebel's Bargain	Annie West
The Million-Dollar Question	Kimberly Lang
Enemies with Benefits	Louisa George
Man vs. Socialite	Charlotte Phillips
Fired by Her Fling	Christy McKellen
The Twelve Dates of Christmas	Susan Meier
At the Chateau for Christmas	Rebecca Winters
A Very Special Holiday Gift	Barbara Hannay
A New Year Marriage Proposal	Kate Hardy
A Little Christmas Magic	Alison Roberts
Christmas with the Maverick Millionaire	Scarlet Wilson

MEDICAL

Playing the Playboy's Sweetheart	Carol Marinelli
Unwrapping Her Italian Doc	Carol Marinelli
A Doctor by Day...	Emily Forbes
Tamed by the Renegade	Emily Forbes

ROMANCE

Christakis's Rebellious Wife	Lynne Graham
At No Man's Command	Melanie Milburne
Carrying the Sheikh's Heir	Lynn Raye Harris
Bound by the Italian's Contract	Janette Kenny
Dante's Unexpected Legacy	Catherine George
A Deal with Demakis	Tara Pammi
The Ultimate Playboy	Maya Blake
Her Irresistible Protector	Michelle Douglas
The Maverick Millionaire	Alison Roberts
The Return of the Rebel	Jennifer Faye
The Tycoon and the Wedding Planner	Kandy Shepherd

HISTORICAL

A Lady of Notoriety	Diane Gaston
The Scarlet Gown	Sarah Mallory
Safe in the Earl's Arms	Liz Tyner
Betrayed, Betrothed and Bedded	Juliet Landon
Castle of the Wolf	Margaret Moore

MEDICAL

200 Harley Street: The Proud Italian	Alison Roberts
200 Harley Street: American Surgeon in London	Lynne Marshall
A Mother's Secret	Scarlet Wilson
Return of Dr Maguire	Judy Campbell
Saving His Little Miracle	Jennifer Taylor
Heatherdale's Shy Nurse	Abigail Gordon

Mills & Boon® Hardback
December 2014

ROMANCE

Taken Over by the Billionaire	Miranda Lee
Christmas in Da Conti's Bed	Sharon Kendrick
His for Revenge	Caitlin Crews
A Rule Worth Breaking	Maggie Cox
What The Greek Wants Most	Maya Blake
The Magnate's Manifesto	Jennifer Hayward
To Claim His Heir by Christmas	Victoria Parker
Heiress's Defiance	Lynn Raye Harris
Nine Month Countdown	Leah Ashton
Bridesmaid with Attitude	Christy McKellen
An Offer She Can't Refuse	Shoma Narayanan
Breaking the Boss's Rules	Nina Milne
Snowbound Surprise for the Billionaire	Michelle Douglas
Christmas Where They Belong	Marion Lennox
Meet Me Under the Mistletoe	Cara Colter
A Diamond in Her Stocking	Kandy Shepherd
Falling for Dr December	Susanne Hampton
Snowbound with the Surgeon	Annie Claydon

MEDICAL

Midwife's Christmas Proposal	Fiona McArthur
Midwife's Mistletoe Baby	Fiona McArthur
A Baby on Her Christmas List	Louisa George
A Family This Christmas	Sue MacKay